Venus Spring

Stunt★Girl

Jonny Zucker writes for children, teenagers and adults. His first novel for Piccadilly was the teen title *One Girl, Two Decks, Three Degrees of Love,* which was serialised by BBC radio. Jonny lives in North London with his wife and young children.

Venus Spring

Stunt☆Girl

JONNY ZUCKER

PICCADILLY PRESS • LONDON

For Fiona, Jake and Ben

First published in Great Britain in 2005
by Piccadilly Press Ltd.,
5 Castle Road, London NW1 8PR
www.piccadillypress.co.uk

A catalogue record for this book is available from the British Library

ISBN: 1 85340 837 9 (trade paperback)

1 3 5 7 9 10 8 6 4 2

Printed and bound in Great Britain by Bookmarque Ltd
Cover design, text design and setting by Simon Davis
Cover illustration by Nicola Taylor

Set in 11.5 point Palatino and Avant Garde

DAY ONE

⚇ Chapter 1

12.40

Venus Spring pushed a branch away from her face and pressed on. Her legs trembled with exhaustion, but determination carried her forward through the thick mud and over jagged stones that clawed into the soles of her trainers. Ahead of her, at the end of the twisting gravel path, she could see the mesh of rope. She'd lost all sense of time now – all she knew was she had to reach it.

The rope net was now only a few metres away. As she got closer she flung herself forward, catching the rope with her left hand while her right thudded against a splintered wooden pole. She winced in pain but began to climb.

Dragging herself upwards, the rope scraped against the palms of her hands and her arm muscles groaned with every movement. It was about ten metres to the

•• | ••

top, but it might as well have been ten thousand. She pulled her shattered body up, reached the summit and struggled on the top of the horizontal beam.

Venus looked at the drop down. Normally she'd plan a jump, work out the angles and mentally prepare, but she didn't have time for thinking. She pushed herself off and fell on to the rough ground below, rolling over to cushion her fall, but still managing to jar her left shoulder. Her body twisted to a halt, her hair and face splashed with flecks of muddy water.

She lay on her back for a second. A part of her wanted to stay there on the ground, gazing up at the clear blue sky. But something deep inside her ruled that option out. However tired she was, Venus wasn't a quitter.

Picking herself up, she spied the river ahead, with the wide wooden bridge crossing from left to right. Not that it was of much use. Most of its slats were submerged under water.

As Venus reached the water's edge, she clenched her teeth and waded straight in, the cold biting into her legs. Her whole body began to shake. She pushed on – the chilled sluices now up to her waist.

Further in she went – the water up to her neck and rising fast. The bridge was now directly in front of her, blocking her way. Venus prepared herself for the only possible strategy for making further progress. The bridge was too low in the water. She'd have to go *under* it. Unfortunately, this would entail submerging herself in the freezing water – a prospect she didn't really relish. Taking a deep breath, Venus plunged her head down into the icy depths. The world suddenly disappeared as she was blinded by the oncoming flow. She swam forward; the water working against her, trying to hold her back with its unrelenting grasp. Despite trying to keep her mouth closed, grit and water swirled past her lips into her throat, making her choke. She struggled on a few more metres. Was she still beneath the bridge? Had she passed under it?

Lurching upwards, she flung her head up out of the water, her lungs greedily grabbing at the fresh air. She coughed violently, found her feet striking land, and stood still for a few seconds, the blood pounding between her ears. She looked down through her sore, streaming eyes. As she surveyed her drenched clothes, the feeling of utter exhaustion swept over her body. She squelched out of the water.

'Not bad,' called a deep, male voice on the bank straight in front of her, 'but next time, I want it fifteen seconds faster.'

🏃 Chapter 2

Selecting the treacherous assault course as the first activity on stunt camp had been a bit on the harsh side. But Dennis Spring wasn't one for easy options. He was the country's top stunt coordinator and stunt artist, and he was renowned for working people very hard. At six foot two, with a well-toned body, scar on his left earlobe, cropped silver hair and wry smile, he cut an imposing figure.

Dennis had repeatedly warned his fourteen-year-old granddaughter, Venus, that she wouldn't be receiving any preferential treatment from him on stunt camp. But when Venus strode out of the icy water to finish the assault course – freezing and shivering – she felt like Dennis was singling her out for *un*preferential treatment.

As Venus changed out of her soaking wet clothes, she found it hard to believe that she was only two hours into stunt camp. It was the first of August and the sun shone through a turquoise sky.

Earlier that day . . .
Dennis had collected everyone from the bus and train stations that morning in his van. On the journey to

Riley Croft people had asked each other's names, but didn't say much else. Venus suspected this was because everyone was feeling the same mix of nerves and excitement that she was experiencing. But Venus had the added worry about the granddad–granddaughter thing. Despite the fact that she'd got her place on camp by merit, would some people think she was only there because she was related to Dennis?

As soon as the van reached the site, the girls and boys immediately piled into their respective dorms. There was a wild buzz of adrenaline and expectation. In the girls' dorm, everyone lunged for the top bunks and Venus was thrilled to secure one. The girls rapid-fired questions at each other. *Where do you come from? What do you reckon camp's going to be like? What's your favourite stunt of all time?*

Venus decided after a few minutes' chatter, that the girls were going to be a top crew. The eight of them seemed to gel almost immediately. They were all there for the same reasons: to learn great stunts and have a laugh. Venus particularly took to Donna – a tall, loud, leather-jacketed girl, with shiny hazel eyes, spiky blond hair and a nose ring. She was a football player and a Manchester United fan. Then there was Jade, a keen runner and long-jumper; Narinder, who was heavily into abseiling and bungee jumping, and Cleo, a swimmer. Polly had a laugh like a hyena and, apparently, kick-boxed as fiercely as Venus. Angie and Mairi seemed more nervous than the others, but they were both experienced athletes and were clearly pleased to be there. All of the girls were fourteen or fifteen apart from sixteen-year-old Cleo.

In the weeks leading up to camp, Venus's best friend and next-door-neighbour, Kate Fox, had complained that while Venus was on stunt camp hanging out with 'gorgeous guys', she'd be enduring a ten-day stint at the 'most boring place on earth' – her cousins' house in Norfolk. The day after they both returned they were going to France for a week with their mums.

'Who says they'll all be gorgeous?' Venus had pointed out. 'There might be some weird, battle-fixated SAS wannabes.'

After the social mayhem of the first hour, Dennis had summoned the boys and girls from their respective dorms to the common room for his official welcome. The common room was a low-slung building, housing battered, late-Seventies armchairs and sofas, a TV, a coffee table with several tatty packs of cards and a pool table.

On first meeting them, a few of the boys *had* come over as a bit weird to Venus. Spike was in the cadets and thought that participation at stunt camp would propel him straight into the British army. Greg and Steve were ju-jitsu enthusiasts. Tariq, Carl and Rob were all runners so they formed a natural trio. Franco was a quiet fifteen-year-old long-jumper, with dark green eyes, bushy eyebrows and a light covering of chin stubble.

And finally there was Jed. A keen runner, he was fourteen, with light blue eyes, a wide, cheeky grin and spiky, light brown gelled hair. Venus found him relaxed, funny and easy to talk to – as well as handsome.

Dennis quickly called for silence and went over the basic ground rules of camp, which included no laptops or Game Boys, only two hours of television permitted a day and no boys in the girls' dorm and vice versa after lights out, and then turned to his 'curfew'.

'You'll need plenty of sleep, if you want to get the most out of camp. So it's lights out at ten – every night.'

There were groans around the common room, but they were quickly silenced by a glare from Dennis.

'If people flout my lights-out rule, they'll come across my more unpleasant side,' he informed them. 'And don't forget – there are loads of others out there who'd jump at the chance of coming here if one of you gets booted out. So ten p.m. is non-negotiable.'

He then made a further announcement.

'In case anyone wonders why my surname is the

same as Venus's, I'll put you straight right away. Her mum is my daughter, and that makes her my granddaughter. But don't go getting any ideas about Venus being the teacher's pet. She'll be treated exactly the same as everyone else and, like all of you, she's here on merit.'

A few people smiled at her and Venus breathed a sigh of relief. Maybe no one would care that she and Dennis were family.

'OK,' said Dennis, 'our first mission is on the assault course. I want you changed and ready in fifteen minutes.'

As everyone filed out of the common room, Donna grabbed Venus's arm. She could barely contain her excitement.

'I can't believe Dennis is your granddad! You must have seen millions of films being made! Which movie stars have you met?'

Venus had decided to be very careful about what personal stunt information she'd share with people on camp – she didn't want to seem like a boaster.

'I've been on some sets,' Venus replied cautiously, 'and met a few actors and actresses.'

'Like who?' Donna's eyes were bulging with expectation.

'No one that famous – I tend to hang out with the

stunt artists – the people whose faces cinema-goers never see.'

'*Go on!*' Donna pleaded. 'You must have met *someone*.'

'OK.' Venus laughed. 'I met Tara Winton last year on *Diamond Spell*.'

'Oh my God!' Donna squealed. 'What was she like? What did you say to her?'

'Er, I said "hi" and she said "hi" back.'

'That's it?' Donna couldn't mask her disappointment.

'The big stars tend to hang out in their trailers until they're called for. And anyway, when they're out and about, it's hard to get near them – they have teams of staff and some have got bodyguards.'

Donna drank in this information, but wanted more. 'What about Dennis? What's he like on set? Is he as bossy as he seems?'

'He's way bossier! This is time off for him. When he's stunt coordinator, he's got all of these people and equipment to organise. At Easter I was on the set of the new Chuck Walters film for a couple of days.'

'You mean *Airborne Sword*?' Donna asked excitedly. 'I read about the making of that. Can't wait till it's released.'

Venus nodded. 'This stunt guy, Rex Lincoln, kept on being late for calls. So Dennis went for him in a big way – barked at him in front of everyone. From then on, Rex was always on set, like, an hour early!'

'Have you ever met Saffron Richie?' Donna asked as they walked back to the dorm. 'I'm dying to know if she's really had a boob job.'

With the group changed into shorts, T-shirts and tracksuits, Dennis led them deep into some woodland. They stopped in front of a high wooden wall at the start of the assault course.

'If any of you are even half-serious about becoming a stunt artist,' Dennis began, 'you'll need to keep your body in excellent shape, all of the time. And that means you'll need to train most days. Training isn't glamorous – it can be boring and exhausting. But you need to keep at it, because your strength and your reflexes aren't optional extras – they can literally save your life. That's why we're starting here. And this won't be our only visit to this assault course in the next ten days. Right, who wants to go first?'

14.45
When everyone had completed the punishing course – with its steep walls to climb, narrow beams to cross and underwater path to negotiate – a lunch of grilled fish, pasta and salad was served in the site canteen. As

people were finishing eating, Dennis announced they'd be shortly going for a six-mile run. A couple of eyebrows were raised in surprise, but Venus knew better.

Dennis was breaking them in gently.

15.30

Venus ran at the back with Donna. Although she was concentrating on her stride, she couldn't help noticing that Jed ran gracefully and smoothly.

Venus enjoyed the run. Her stamina levels were high and her body felt on good form.

Camp is going to be excellent – totally excellent.

However, if Venus had known for one second about the chain of events that would unfold over the coming days, she wouldn't have felt good at all.

She'd have been overcome with shock and disbelief.

Chapter 3

From a very early age Venus had been a livewire. Her boundless energy got her walking and running well before most of her peers. An only child, she was bright, friendly and very independent. She did well at school, especially in English and PE and developed into a very talented gymnast and runner.

She was striking looking, with large brown eyes and lush, flowing brown hair. She'd never bought into the teen magazines 'perfect girl' look and hated the pressure heaped on girls to diet. But she ate sensibly and for maximum energy. After all, if she was ever going to make it as a professional stunt artist, her body would be her number one asset. So Venus was trim without being a waif and had well-toned muscles without resembling a body builder.

Most of the time Venus wore jeans and T-shirts, but she was more than happy to do slinky skirts, crop tops and experimental hairstyles for parties. And it was rare for Venus to hit a party without Kate, who'd spent hours helping Venus choose what to wear on the journey to Riley Croft. She had wanted to get the right balance – laid-back teenage female mixed with all-action stunt girl. She'd finally settled on a pair of faded jeans, a long-sleeved white T-shirt and trainers.

Kate was sixteen, a computer genius and a fine runner herself. Kate was of a similar height and build to Venus, with light green eyes and straight straw-berry-blond hair. Kate was a great sounding board for Venus – she was a good listener and offered excellent advice. In turn, Kate went to Venus when she had problems that needed sorting out. Their mothers were also very close friends, and the four of them were forever in and out of each other's houses.

Another frequent visitor to Venus's house was Dennis. He was a total Londoner too, having lived in the capital for over thirty years, but he never forgot his roots. Venus loved listening to him talk about his childhood in the West Indies – the sights, the smells, and the colours. In the Sixties, Dennis, his wife Doreen and their young daughter left Trinidad for England – in search of better job opportunities. Doreen was already a skilled midwife and found work quickly. Dennis drove a minicab by day and packed crates of beer by night. But then, through a chance meeting he was offered three days' work as an extra on a film. While on the set, he got talking to the film's stunt coordinator, who was interested in the boxing and athletics Dennis had been involved with in Trinidad. The guy said he was looking to train a new stuntman.

Dennis took up the offer and never looked back.

Dennis and Doreen's daughter Gail was a cheerful, outgoing girl. She excelled at school and studied law at university. She grew up to be a tall, slender woman with light brown eyes and sleek, straight black hair, who was never short of male admirers. Four years after law school, she became the youngest partner in a highly respected firm of family lawyers. In her early thirties she met fellow lawyer, Elliot Nevis, an

•• 13 ••

American living in London. Before Gail knew it, she and Elliot were sharing a house and she was expecting a baby. However, when Gail was six months' pregnant, her mum was diagnosed with cancer and died four weeks later.

And when Venus was just three months old, Elliot suddenly announced he'd made a 'mistake' in becoming a father. He left Gail and Venus and headed back to the States. Shortly after his departure, he wrote to Gail and offered to pay maintenance for Venus. Gail didn't respond to the letter.

All Venus had of her dad was a grainy black and white photo showing the three of them. Gail didn't know about the photo. Venus had found it in the attic when she was eight and kept it in her bedroom cupboard – well-hidden behind a mound of art materials.

Elliot's expression seemed outwardly happy in the photo but, having looked at it thousands of times, Venus was sure she could detect a glint of uncertainty, perhaps even fear, in his eyes. Had he known when the photo was taken that in a matter of weeks he would be out of their lives? Was he already planning his escape from fatherhood? Or did something suddenly happen to make him flee?

Gail rarely spoke to Venus about Elliot. If he ever cropped up in conversations – always initiated by

Venus – Gail referred to him as 'your father', as if she couldn't bear to say his name. Venus's lack of knowledge about Elliot frustrated her and she'd made a promise to herself.

One day, she was going to uncover the full story about her dad.

Chapter 4

21.05

After supper on Day One, Venus found herself in the canteen kitchen with Jed.

For the entire duration of camp, participants (under Dennis's supervision) would be preparing and making all of the meals themselves, with the exception of that first day's lunch and supper which Dennis had provided.

Venus sometimes cooked for herself and her mum at home, but at least half of the people on camp hadn't progressed beyond pouring milk on cereal. Cooking duty for them was going to be a steep learning curve. The washing up was also to be done by the group and Dennis had selected Venus and Jed for the first night's duty.

Venus scrubbed some tomato sauce off a plate and handed it to Jed for drying.

'Top day wasn't it?' Jed smiled.

'Brilliant,' Venus replied. 'The assault course was pretty intense.'

Jed laughed. 'That is so true! I thought I was going to drown under that bridge.'

'Me too – it was like being on one of those desert island survival shows.'

Venus leaned over and passed Jed a stack of bowls. He was definitely cute and his smile was amazing.

The kitchen door suddenly flew open and Dennis strode in purposefully. 'Haven't you two finished yet? At this rate you'll be at that sink all night.'

'We're nearly there,' Venus replied.

'Good,' said Dennis, nodding. 'I want to lock up.'

Venus grinned. 'Message received.'

'Anyway, you both need to get some sleep and prepare yourselves for tomorrow morning.'

They both looked at him with interest. 'What's happening tomorrow morning?' asked Jed, putting some mugs away.

'Wait and see.' Dennis chuckled. 'You won't be disappointed.'

Venus had been fascinated by Dennis's work for as long as she could remember, but it was only when she started secondary school that she decided she wanted to become a top stuntwoman. It made complete sense to her – she loved films, was very sporty and thrived on the thrill of exciting challenges. But she told nothing of this aspiration to her mum or granddad, because they would only worry.

In the New Year, she innocently asked her mum if she could spend part of that year's summer holiday with Dennis at work. She'd been on a couple of sets before, but each time with her mum and only for a few hours. Gail was initially very resistant to this idea. What if Venus was mowed down by an out-of-control vehicle or struck by flying glass? But Dennis was delighted that his granddaughter wanted to spend more time with him, even though he knew how busy he was on film shoots.

So grandfather and granddaughter formed a unit.

'I'll keep a close eye on her,' Dennis promised.

And Venus assured both of them that she'd spend her days on set peacefully – watching scenes being filmed from a safe distance, reading and relaxing. Gail eventually gave in. After all, it was free childcare and she trusted Dennis.

So that summer Venus visited the set of *Tiger Mountain* – a film about a team of law enforcers sent to the Indian jungle to track down a gang of tiger hunters. Venus couldn't believe how authentic the rainforest looked, when in reality it was a set that only filled a quarter of a film studio. In the first week, Venus watched, listened and kept well back. But at the start of the second week, she revealed her great career plan to Dennis. The stunt world was for her and she wanted to get started with her training right now. Could he please teach her some stunts?

At first, Dennis refused point-blank. 'Your mum will never, ever go for it,' he said. 'It's a total non-starter. She'd kill me.'

'But Mum doesn't need to know,' Venus replied, 'and if she doesn't know she can't give you a hard time.'

Dennis stood firm, but Venus was extremely persuasive and after two days of constant badgering his resolve was finally broken.

'OK, OK,' he reluctantly conceded. 'I'll show you some stuff when things are quiet. And even though I'm going against my better instinct, I agree that we keep it secret from your mum. It's just not worth going there. However, we only do the most basic moves. I'm not having you jumping off any high water tanks.'

A week later, after Venus had jumped off a high water tank, Dennis entertained the possibility that his granddaughter might just have got the better of him.

And as time passed and Venus visited more sets, Dennis taught Venus increasingly challenging stunts:

from key fight moves, via shimmying up a rope in seconds, to the best method of avoiding a collapsing brick wall. It was during a Christmas holiday, on the set of *War Tribe* – a film set in a futuristic hell – that twelve-year-old Venus first learned to drive. Dennis hadn't wanted to let her anywhere near a vehicle, but he relented when she promised to accept his supervision at extremely close proximity.

'Get your hands off the wheel,' Venus yelled at him as she got to grips with steering a Land Rover through a giant dust bowl at seventy miles an hour.

'You're twelve, Venus!' Dennis had yelled back, pulling at the wheel even harder.

'I don't care – you're making me swerve!'

'If I wasn't making you swerve, you'd crash and I'd end up paying for the car!'

Along the way, there were certain ideas that Dennis drilled into Venus.

'Never, ever rely on someone else to check your harness, crash mat or other piece of safety equipment,' he was always telling her. 'Check them yourself and then check them again. That way if something doesn't work, the only person to blame if something goes wrong is you.'

Venus took all of Dennis's advice very seriously, but sometimes she couldn't help getting a bit carried away with all of the exhilaration as she completed a fall or dived through a narrow piece of steel tubing. She'd imagine herself as a body double for Saffron Richie or Tara Winton, flying over a ship's rigging as a swash-buckling pirate or scaling Big Ben as a deadly secret agent. But Dennis would always bring her back down to earth. 'Don't disappear into a dream world, Venus. You're not in the movies yet. Keep both feet firmly on the ground, here in reality.'

Venus watched films with completely different eyes from anyone she knew – with the exception of Dennis. She'd replay stunt scenes on the DVD player over and over in slow motion, looking at the positioning and movements of the stunt artists.

Venus's stunt heroine was Kelly Tanner. They had never met, but Dennis had worked with Kelly several times and often told Venus she was the best in the business. Kelly was famous for the helicopter jump in *Point Turn*, but Venus could cite so many other examples of her brilliance, like the laser battle in *Space Force 2424* or the ramparts escape from the burning castle in *Joust*. Venus begged Dennis to work with Kelly again so she could meet her. But nowadays Kelly lived and worked mainly in Los Angeles. In Venus's dreamworld, she wouldn't merely follow in Kelly Tanner's footsteps. She'd *be* Kelly.

When Gail asked how she'd spent her days on sets, Venus always gave vague answers about 'hanging out' and 'doing my own thing'. Venus felt incredibly guilty about lying to her mum, but she couldn't see any way round it. She was dead set on becoming a top stunt artist and there was no way Gail would go for that as a career option for her only daughter.

Venus told Kate everything. And Kate was brilliant at keeping secrets.

So Venus ended up leading a double life. On the surface she was Venus Spring, the school student, athlete and music fan. But the minute she walked through the security barrier at a film studio or shoot location, she became Venus Spring, Stunt Girl.

As Venus's fourteenth birthday loomed, she casually told her mum she'd like to go to Dennis's annual stunt camp for fourteen- to sixteen-year-olds. Gail was surprised by this request. 'I know you like watching Dennis at work, but you've never mentioned you want to do stunts *yourself*.'

'It's good to try out new things – it could be fun.'

Venus cringed as the words came out of her mouth. What a major lie!

Gail questioned Dennis in detail about his camp. *Would Venus get hurt? What sort of kids would she be mixing with? Who'd be doing the cooking? Were the toilets clean?* Dennis fielded these questions superbly and told Venus that Gail would come round to the idea sooner or later.

It took a while. But in the end, after a lot of badgering, Venus got the result she wanted.

🏃 Chapter 5

21.45

'Well? How was your first day?' It was Venus's mum calling on her mobile.

After Venus and Jed had finished washing up, they'd gone to the common room to hang out with the others, but now it was time for bed. No one was keen to break Dennis's curfew – at least not on the first night.

Venus was wearing her black with white dots pyjama shorts and vest top. It was a warm night. She slipped out of the dorm with her mobile.

'It's good, Mum.'

'Have you eaten properly?'

'Yes.'

'Are the others nice?'

'They're fine.'

'Are the showers OK?'

'They're passable.'

'And the toilets?'

'Mum, stop worrying.'

'I'm your mother, Venus. I'm *programmed* to worry.'

Venus laughed.

'So you think it's going to be good?'

'It's going to be great, Mum, but I need to go back into the dorm. If Dennis catches me out here, I'm dead.'

'Of course, he can be a bit strict can't he?'

'A bit?'

'OK, off you go. I'll call you soon.'

21.47

Seventy miles away, a woman with silver eyes and short blond hair was walking briskly down a quiet city street. She strolled past a greasy spoon café and an off-licence. Further down the street, a neon sign swung in the wind over the entrance to a white, Georgian three-storey building. *Hotel Sable*, the sign declared.

The woman walked past the sign, checked over her shoulder and then slipped down a narrow alleyway. Fifty metres down, the alley curved to the left. This took her round to the narrow strip of a gravel car park at the back of the hotel. She crossed the car park and walked down a flight of stone steps to a courtyard below. Facing her, across the courtyard was another flight of steps.

She didn't have to wait long.

Footsteps sounded from above the courtyard and a man appeared at the top of the second flight. He wore a long, black leather coat, a beige beanie hat and thin-framed sunglasses. He descended the steps and crossed over to her.

'Have you got it?' she asked.

He held a tightly clenched fist. 'And the first payment?' he demanded.

'They'll have the money tonight.'

He pursed his lips and slowly unfolded his fist. On his outstretched palm was a small gold key with the number thirty-one etched on its surface.

She took the key and held it up for inspection. The man whispered something quickly. She memorised it. He then slunk back across the courtyard, up the steps and out of sight. The woman slipped the key into her handbag and headed back the way she came.

DAY TWO

🏃 Chapter 6

07.30

When Venus woke up, everyone was asleep in the girls' dorm apart from Polly and Cleo who were heading for the showers. Venus walked out of the dorm and leaned against the wooden railing on the veranda. She savoured the view as her eyes took in the great expanse of the site.

It was a very quiet part of the Devonshire countryside. Once there had been an air force base, so Dennis told them on the drive from the station, but it was no longer in use. Apart from the camp's dorms, classroom, canteen, site office and equipment store, the only other buildings of any significance in the vicinity belonged to Docker's farm, owned and run by Alan Docker. Being such a regular visitor to the area, Dennis and Alan had become good friends over the years.

As Venus stood looking out across the site, she

saw a tractor pull up outside the site office. Dennis emerged, calling, 'Good morning, Alan!'

This was followed by a shout from Dennis who'd spotted Venus standing on the veranda. 'Venus, come here a second!'

Venus walked over and Dennis introduced her to Alan. He was a large man with tousled salt-and-pepper hair, ruddy cheeks and a warm smile on his lips. He shook her hand heartily.

'So finally I get to meet your granddaughter!' Alan said.

Venus sat down with them at a wooden table outside the Portakabin office. At first Alan steered the conversation towards her, asking about school and her friends, but then he started talking about tractor sales, the trouble they'd had with poachers Joe Thorn and Arthur Simmons, greedy developers wanting his land and fox-hunting. He then talked with pride about his seven-year-old-daughter Annie who was learning to swim in the lake on the farm. Venus listened patiently for a while, but was relieved when Donna stuck her head out of the girls' dorm window and called to her.

'Venus, get in here now! Polly's about to tell us how she dumped her last boyfriend.'

Venus stood up. 'Gotta go,' she said.

'Make sure Dennis goes easy on you,' said Alan.

'There'll be no preferential treatment round here,' Dennis insisted with a wink at his granddaughter.

Venus smiled, rolled her eyes to the heavens and walked back to the girls' dorm, where everyone was sitting expectantly around Polly.

🏃 Chapter 7

08.25

'I'm your wake-up call.'

'I've just finished breakfast, Kate.'

'OK, I'm your *after breakfast* call. How's it going, Venus?'

'Good – how's your cousins' place?'

'Think of hell and multiply it by fifty. They are so boring! If I have to play another game of Scrabble, I'll eat their carpet!'

Venus laughed. 'You usually hate it at the start, but it's always OK in the end.'

'Bring on the end, then,' Kate moaned. 'Anyway, what are the others like? Any cute boys?'

'Nah.'

'Shame.'

'Well . . .'

'Yeah?'

'There – there is this boy called Jed . . .'

'OK.'

'He's cute, but I reckon all the girls like him.'

'But you're not the other girls, Venus. Check him out.'

Venus laughed again. 'Whatever. Anyway, gotta go, we're starting soon.'

'Cool. Just pray for sunshine so I can escape the dreaded Scrabble board.'

'Will do.'

'Catch ya later.'

09.00

'The idea behind circuits,' Dennis explained, 'is that you use different muscle groups for different tasks. That way, you can build your fitness gradually without asking too much of any single part of your body.'

The group were standing on the site's football pitch, looking at the activities set up around them. Dennis went over each 'station' carefully – the rope climb, the bench presses, the free weights, the running and the vaulting. The group worked in twenty-minute sessions, with three-minute breaks in between. By the end of the fourth complete circuit, Steve, Narinder and Mairi were starting to feel the strain.

'I thought I was fit,' whispered Donna to Venus, 'but my body seems to be disassembling itself!'

'Look at you!' Dennis grinned at the group. 'I haven't even started yet!'

13.20

After lunch, Dennis played them a short DVD of classic fight scenes, including Kelly Tanner doubling for Tara Winton in *Sky Trooper*'s cliff-top fight with the devil. Venus knew the moves by heart.

'The best stunt artists make fighting look easy, but it isn't,' Dennis told them at the end of the DVD. 'You have to convince the audience that you really are exchanging blows and that every time you're hit it hurts.'

The rest of the afternoon was filled by people practising their fake punches, blocks and falls, with occasional bouts of laughter and one or two accidental hits reaching their targets. Venus sparred with Tariq, Polly and Spike, although she did find her eyes wandering approvingly in Jed's direction several times.

20.45

After supper, lots of people drifted back to the dorms, to get a decent night's sleep. Venus, Donna and Jed went to the common room to hang out. Greg and Steve were the only two people there – they were playing pool.

Venus had let her hair down and was wearing boot-cut jeans and a purple fleece. She'd noticed Jed's look of approval when she sat down next to him at supper.

'My feet have lost all sensation.' Donna winced dramatically, flopping into an armchair.

Venus smiled and took a sip from her bottle of water. 'In the hand-to-hand, I nearly got whacked by Polly when I wasn't looking, but I ducked at the last second and she fell on top of Tariq.'

Donna and Jed laughed. 'What do you reckon we're doing tomorrow?' asked Donna.

'Absolutely no idea,' Venus replied, 'but knowing Dennis it will be harder than today.'

'No wonder you fight so well, Venus,' Jed said with a wink, 'it must run in the family.'

Venus nodded her head in a mock bow to accept the compliment.

21.30

With Dennis's curfew approaching, the five in the common room decided to head for bed. They were nearly back at the dorms when Venus felt in her jacket pocket and realised she'd left her torch in the canteen.

'It's on one of the tables,' she said. 'I forgot to pick it up after supper.'

'Do you want me to walk you back?' Jed asked.

'Na, it's cool,' Venus replied, though she felt flattered by the offer.

Not just handsome, but chivalrous as well!

'OK, see you in a minute,' Donna said, waving.

When Venus got to the canteen, she found it dark, empty, silent and locked. Dennis was big on security. She sighed, but it was no big deal – she'd get it at breakfast. She was about to turn and walk back to the dorm when she noticed something further down the path. The tiniest crack of light was spilling under the door of an old outhouse. This building leaned slightly and its brickwork had seen far better days. Gaps showed amongst the slate roofing tiles. A large *Danger – Keep Out* board with a hard-hat emblem was hung above the door.

Venus stood still for a minute. The outhouse wasn't used for anything. Dennis had told them yesterday that the building wasn't safe and would be demolished in the near future. So why was there a light in there? It didn't make any sense. The warmth of the girls' dorm beckoned, but Venus was intrigued. She crept forwards to the end of the path and ever so lightly pressed her face against the outhouse door, gaining a tiny strip of vision.

Inside, Franco was sitting on the straw-covered floor, cross-legged, with his back to the door; a laptop balanced on his knees. Beside him was a folded-out map. He wore a serious expression on his face, reflected in the light from the laptop screen.

Venus watched him silently. *No laptops on camp* was one of Dennis's big rules. 'They're a total distraction,' he'd written in the brochure.

Venus watched as Franco clicked the mouse. There was another map on-screen. He scrolled down, stopped and enlarged what looked like a stretch of water. As Venus looked on, she remembered there was a beach less than fifteen miles from Riley Croft.

Very carefully, she slid her fingertips around the edge of the door and pulled it open a fraction further, to get a better view. As she did this, her right foot knocked a pebble that in turn brushed against the wooden door, making a tiny thud. In a split second, the laptop light was extinguished. She leaped back.

A few moments later, the door swung open and Franco stepped outside. He stood silently, staring into the night, swivelling his head for signs of any movement. He moved forward, pushed the folded map into one of the pockets of his combats and looked up at the outhouse roof. It was illuminated by silver threads of moonlight, but was still and quiet. He shook his head and retreated quickly back inside, pulling the door tightly shut behind him. A few seconds later, a tiny ray of light beneath the door appeared again.

Three metres away, Venus lay still in the long damp grass. She'd hidden because she didn't want Franco to think she was spying on him. She couldn't help wondering what he was doing in there. *He's probably just an Internet junkie who can't live without his daily fix of web hits. The outhouse could be his secret logging on venue, away from the prying eyes of other people, namely Dennis,* she thought.

She waited a couple of minutes before standing up and walking back to the girls' dorm.

'What took you so long?' asked Donna, who was lying on her bed writing a postcard by torchlight.

'Canteen was locked,' Venus replied. 'I tried to get in through a window, but it was impossible.'

'It's night-time, Venus. Switch off from stunt mode. Use the door tomorrow!'

'Yeah, I will,' Venus replied with a grin. 'Just going to brush my teeth.'

Venus thought about Franco using the laptop as she walked to the shower block. *Why was he looking at a stretch of water? Did the two maps feature the same area?*

She brushed her teeth and looked in the mirror.

Is it somewhere round here?

She reached up to turn off the shower block light.

It's nothing. Just chill out.

DAY THREE

🏃 Chapter 8

14.30

'OK,' Dennis said, 'I want you all to listen very carefully.'

The whole morning had been taken up with team-building activities: carrying a heavy rucksack from one destination to another using only branches; getting through a dense area of woodland with their feet tied together; completing a lightning-quick treasure hunt, complete with fighting off opposing teams. Venus had been in a group with Greg, Polly and Narinder and they'd worked brilliantly together.

Everyone was now standing behind the football pitch, staring up at a series of wooden beams, horizontal ladders, rope bridges and a range of steps, large and small. The equipment was all connected between trees that formed a huge circle around them. It was a mid-air racetrack. Beneath the track was an enormous stretch of taut netting. Everyone was wearing a helmet.

The group stood silently, eyes fixed on Dennis.

'You'll be going round in pairs. One of you will be the chased, and the other the chaser. There is a set way round and the start is the square wooden platform at the top of the cut-off tree over there. The end is the firefighter pole. The chased has to get to the bottom of that pole without being tagged by the chaser. The chased gets a fifteen-second head start.'

A few people shuffled their feet in anticipation.

'There's plenty of room up there, so we'll have three pairs on the go at any one time.'

Venus scanned the equipment, looking for weak spots and opportunities to speed up. Dennis had instilled into her the need for rigorous observation before any stunt.

Polly and Cleo were chosen to go first. They climbed the footholds on the tree and stood together on the platform.

'OK,' called Dennis, looking at his watch. 'Polly, you've got the head start. One, two, three . . . Go!'

Ten minutes later, Venus was craning her neck to watch Donna and Spike's chase, when Dennis called her and Jed over for their turn. She was to be the chased.

Venus walked to the tree and put her foot on the

first foothold. She climbed up, with Jed close behind her. They stood together on the platform.

'May the best woman win,' Venus said, holding out her palm.

Jed slapped it. 'I'll get you before you're halfway round,' he said with a grin.

Venus laughed. 'In your dreams.'

Dennis called out from below. 'All right Venus, One, two, three . . . Go!'

Venus leaped forward like a frenzied horse being released from its starting gate at a racetrack. She flew across the first wooden beam and over a short rope bridge.

'OK, Jed,' she heard Dennis shout. 'Go!'

Venus clambered up and over a short flight of wooden stairs jumping down and landing on a slatted wooden walkway. She could hear Jed's footsteps crashing behind her. She grabbed the metal beams above her and swung forward. Jed was gaining on her.

Along another even narrower beam she sped and on to a second rope bridge. Stepping over it speedily, her foot slipped and her leg nearly fell through a gap. But she steadied herself and jumped forward onto the next platform.

She leaped across a series of giant metal stepping stones. Risking a glance behind, she saw that Jed was closing the gap. She sped on, over a horizontal ladder. Jed was now almost within tagging distance. Venus upped her pace but Jed matched her. The end was now in sight but, before she reached the firefighter pole, she had to navigate a wide gap. The only way to cross it was to use the rope hanging down over it. Her mind whirred. Reaching out for the rope would cost her a couple of seconds, plenty of time for Jed to get her.

She hurtled along a wooden beam towards the rope. She looked around quickly. Jed was reaching out to touch her. She pulled her shoulder just out of his grasp and held out her arms as if to grab the rope.

It was a very long shot, but Venus was well used to working out the percentages. She'd often watched the long-jumpers at the Olympics – studying the shapes their bodies made as they hurled themselves.

Venus leaped from the platform like a springing cheetah, pumping her legs as she'd seen long-jumpers do. There were gasps from people below – there was no way she could make it across without the rope. She hung in the air as if for a split second she'd bypassed the laws of time and gravity.

Jed snatched at the rope and swung.

Suddenly back in normal time, the toes of Venus's trainers connected with the edge of the wooden circle on the other side.

Jed was speeding through the air towards her. He let go of the rope and flew forward. But Venus was too quick. She jumped forward and slid down the pole. Reaching the ground she felt the electric fizz of elation. She'd done it! She punched the air. A second later Jed landed at the bottom of the pole.

'You were incredible up there,' he said, panting. 'I really thought I'd got you.'

'Cheers.' She smiled, the praise singing in her ears. 'You weren't too bad yourself.'

16.07

Venus and Jed were sitting on the canteen steps, comparing bruises.

'I'll get you next time,' Jed said.

'You wish,' Venus answered with a grin. 'You were nowhere near me!'

'I so nearly got you!' Jed protested.

They were quiet for a while, looking across at the small group who were trying to build their suntans on the grass in front of the dorms.

'What do you make of Franco?' Jed suddenly asked.

An image of Franco and his outhouse laptop session flicked through Venus's mind. She thought for a moment about telling Jed, but decided against it. 'He's OK,' she replied. 'A bit quiet.'

'Did you notice how he sat apart from the rest of us during the high-wire activity?'

Venus shook her head.

'I've tried talking to him several times,' Jed continued, 'and it's almost impossible to get an answer. I think he's a bit weird.'

Venus thought about this for a second. 'Maybe he's just shy – some people are like that. Perhaps he'll warm up later in the week.'

'Maybe.' Jed nodded, but he didn't look very convinced.

🏃 Chapter 9

18.45

'The indoor tennis courts are being refurbished and will be open again to members in two weeks.'

The spotty young man with over-gelled hair and an ID badge stating his name, Richard Kelton, looked into the woman's silver eyes with eager anticipation. He noted her smooth, black hair and long eyelashes. She looked very well kempt. She was bound to be wealthy. He was certain she was going to sign up for a year's membership of the Fitness Central Health Club, which meant a bonus for him.

'OK,' Richard continued. 'Why don't we crack on with the tour and then we can come back over here to do the membership forms and set up your direct debit.'

'That's an excellent idea.' She smiled warmly.

At the end of the tour, they stood outside the women's changing rooms.

'Obviously, I'm not allowed inside there,' Richard explained, 'but go on in and check out the facilities. I'll wait here for you.'

She nodded, pushed open the door and found herself in a large rectangular changing room. There was no one else inside. The woman extracted the small gold key from her trouser pocket and inserted it into the keyhole of locker number thirty-one. The door swung open. At the back was a small square of paper. She reached for it quickly.

Floor 5 Parchment Buildings. Night Fire Technology.

Placing the piece of paper in her wallet, she reached for a business card in her pocket and dialled a number on her mobile.

'Richard Kelton speaking,' answered the voice.

'There's a parcel for you at the front entrance,' she said with an American twang.

'What sort of parcel?'

'It's some sort of cash prize.'

'OK,' Richard Kelton said, 'I'll be there in twenty seconds.'

She stuffed her black wig and false eyelashes into her bag and gave him ten seconds before leaving the changing room. The corridor was empty. She made her way out of a side door and strolled round to the front of the club. Just inside the front entrance, she saw Richard Kelton shouting at a bemused-looking receptionist about a prize that had just been delivered for him.

The silver-eyed woman turned and dissappeared into the bustle of people on the high street.

DAY FOUR

🏃 Chapter 10

09.50

Venus leaned out over the edge of a platform, studying the twenty-metre drop in front. The platform was at the top of a wooden tower and below was a huge blue crash mat, beside which stood Dennis with a clipboard.

Venus was one of the few to have done a jump like this before, but most of the others had some experience of abseiling or climbing, so no one was completely freaking out. Donna, however, was chewing her nails a little anxiously.

'I'm not great with heights,' she whispered to Venus.

'Pin your arms as close to your body as possible,' Dennis shouted up at them. 'The more compact you are, the safer you fall. Check and recheck your stance and positioning. Any of you who've seen *The Kite Chaser* will know that incredible jump Angie Carlo makes off the Spanish watchtower. Looked amazing, didn't it? Well, what you don't know is that the stuntwoman doubling for Angie – Carly Fisher – got a bit too confident. She didn't prepare herself properly – skipped some of her safety checks before the jump. Result? The stunt looked fantastic, but Carly picked up a broken arm and two broken legs.'

'Thanks for that,' mumbled Donna, turning slightly pale.

'Any questions?' shouted Dennis.

There was silence up on the platform.

'I bet he makes me go first,' Donna muttered.

'He won't,' replied Venus.

'Right,' shouted Dennis, 'Donna, you're first.'

Donna groaned. 'I told you. First off and first to die!'

'You'll be fine,' said Venus, squeezing her on the shoulder. 'Go girl!'

Donna's jump was OK and Venus watched as the others took their turns. Jade, Steve and Tariq were spot on, while a few fell a bit awkwardly. Dennis took the latter ones aside and gave them quick one-to-one tutorials. The last were Venus and Franco.

Franco stood back and folded his arms.

'I guess I'll go first,' said Venus.

Franco shrugged his shoulders. Venus closed her

eyes for a few seconds to mentally prepare herself. She tucked her arms tightly into her sides. It was time for the leap. She pushed off with her trainers and moved forward. But, reaching the edge, she stumbled over something and lurched forward, almost falling. She just managed to steady herself and arched backwards on to the platform. She looked, but saw nothing obstructing the floorboards.

Franco stood a few paces behind her.

She looked at his expressionless face for a few seconds. She'd double-checked her laces and looked for stones on the platform before starting her jump. Jed's remark last night that Franco was 'a bit weird' quickly flashed through her mind. Could Franco have seen her outside the old outhouse? Maybe he'd tripped her to warn her off? This possibility made Venus feel uneasy. She gave him a quick glance. Surely he wouldn't do anything like that?

'Get on with it, Venus!' called Dennis.

Venus pushed the thought away, stepped forward and leaped off the platform.

21.20

After supper everyone was in the common room. The afternoon had been challenging – more circuits and a longer run. Most people were watching a football match on TV, but Venus found it hard to concentrate. She kept on thinking about Franco's furtive laptop session and her 'trip' on the platform. Putting these two events together made Venus feel a nagging twinge of discomfort. There was definitely something odd about him.

When Dennis poked his head around the door to tell everyone it was nine forty-five, Venus got up off the sofa. She casually strolled out after him and caught him up halfway along the path.

'All right, Venus?' He smiled. 'You're doing great. Are you enjoying it?'

'It's brilliant! I especially liked the high chase.'

He put his arm around her and gave her a side hug. 'And I love having you here, kid – I'm really proud of you.'

Venus looked around to make sure no one was within earshot. 'Granddad, there's something I wanted to ask you.'

'Yes?'

'I was wondering what you know about Franco?'

Dennis stared at her with a puzzled expression. 'What do you want to know?'

'Just stuff.'

'Why the interest in Franco?'

'You know me, I'm Queen Nosy.'

'He seems a bit remote,' Dennis replied, 'but OK. The only information I have about him is on his application form. Those forms are in a cabinet in the site office – and they're strictly confidential.'

'Yeah, of course.' Venus smiled.

'If there's something you want to know, why don't you just ask him?'

'Course I will – anyway it so doesn't matter.'

'Are you sure, Venus? Is there something on your mind?'

Venus laughed. 'No, it's nothing, forget it.'

'Whatever you say kid,' he replied, stooping down to kiss her on the forehead. 'Now if you're going back to the common room, tell everyone it's lights out in ten minutes.'

'OK, Granddad.'

'And remind them about my nasty streak!'

DAY FIVE

🏃 Chapter 11

08.17

'Hi, Kate.'

'Whassup?'

Venus was waiting outside the shower block for Polly and Cleo to finish. 'I'm getting a bad vibe about a guy here called Franco,' she whispered.

'What sort of bad vibe?'

'I saw him the other night in this crumbling out-house looking at a laptop in private – they're banned.'

'Venus! Using a laptop in an outhouse or anywhere else isn't a crime. Anyway, what did you say to him?'

'Nothing. I just watched him.'

'You mean you spied on him?'

'No . . . yes . . . sort of. I didn't mean to, but he looked really suspicious. I've asked Dennis, but he wouldn't tell me anything about Franco.'

'Of course not! You wouldn't want any of the others knowing your personal details, would you?'

'No, I suppose not, but there is something else. I stumbled just before I did a jump yesterday. You know I do all of my checks properly. There was nothing on the platform to trip me up. And guess who was the only other person up there?'

Kate groaned. 'Venus, what are you like? You're on a *summer camp*. You probably just slipped. Save the conspiracy theories for your first action movie.'

'I dunno, Kate . . .'

'Venus,' Kate said, sighing heavily. 'It's nothing. Pack away that mad imagination of yours and get on with having a laugh.'

'So tell me,' Venus went on, quickly changing the subject, 'how's it going at your end?'

'We had a Scrabble marathon last night.' Kate replied, groaning.

'Nightmare.'

'It wasn't that bad – I won.'

Venus laughed. 'Let's speak soon?'

'Cool. And Venus?'

'Yes?'

'No more spying.'

'Sure.'

Venus flicked her hair out of her face and shielded her eyes from the sun. She was wearing shorts and a white vest top. The sun was beating down as she, Donna, Cleo, Jed and Tariq lay on the grass next to the site equipment store. They'd just finished a session on chasing and apprehending. Venus had dodged several would-be assailants, imagining she was doubling for Saffron Richie on the set of a major motion picture.

'How much do you reckon Kelly Tanner earns in a year?' asked Donna.

'Stacks,' replied Tariq, chewing a blade of grass. 'But nowhere near as much as the guys.'

'You're joking, right?' asked Cleo.

'No way,' Tariq insisted. 'No disrespect to women, but the men perform far harder and more dangerous stunts.'

Venus couldn't let this go. 'Kelly's actually done a couple of stunts men weren't prepared to do,' she said.

'Name one!' answered Tariq, now on the defensive.

'You know in *Land of the Delta* – that bit where Dave Roddy bikes off the cliff?'

'Yeah.' Tariq nodded.

'Well, the two main male stunt doubles refused to do it.'

'You're joking?' Tariq responded.

Venus shook her head. 'It's totally true. Kelly stepped in.'

'Good one, Venus,' Donna said with a laugh, giving Venus the thumbs up.

'I'd work in the movies for free,' said Cleo.

'Yeah, me too,' agreed Jed.

'I wouldn't,' said Donna. 'I need the cash!'

'Anyway, better get a move on. The girls versus boys football match is about to start,' Jed said.

He stood and held out his hand. Venus took it and he pulled her up from the ground. For a second their hands stayed clasped and their eyes locked, but Spike walked over and grabbed Jed by the arm, dragging him towards the football pitch.

'Come on, Venus,' Jed called over his shoulder, 'you girls don't stand a chance!'

16.20

The game ended 2-2. Everyone had joined in apart from Franco, who spent most of the time on the touchline, watching. After the match, Venus was hanging out on the veranda outside the girls' dorm with Donna and Cleo. Donna was braiding Cleo's hair when Venus's mobile rang.

'Mum.'

'There was a thing on the radio this afternoon about

a shock flash flood somewhere in Devon. It wasn't anywhere near you, was it?'

'No. The weather's gorgeous here. I've just been playing footy.'

'Hi, Mrs Spring,' Donna called out.

'Who was that?' asked Venus's mum.

'It's my new mate, Donna. Anyway, how are you, Mum?'

'Oh you know,' she said with a laugh, 'tired, underpaid.'

'They work you too hard, Mum.'

'I know, honey, but I love it really. So things are still going well down there?'

'Yeah – it's excellent.'

'The house is pretty quiet without you.'

'But you do get the whole sofa to yourself,' Venus reminded her.

'I wasn't going to say that, but now that you mention it . . .'

'Enjoy it while you can, Mum. I'll claim back my half when I get home!'

Just then, Venus noticed Jed walk out in front of the dining hall. He winked at her.

'Why did I know you were going to say that?' said Gail.

'Hey, Mum. I've got to go. Catch you later. Ciao.'

🏃 Chapter 12

Dennis was about to make a call in the site office, when he heard his name being called. It was Jed. He was sitting at the side of the path, holding his right foot, with an agonised expression on his face.

'What's up?' Dennis called, walking quickly towards him.

'I twisted my ankle in the football match.' Jed winced. 'It was OK for a bit, but I just knocked it again and now it's really painful.'

'Let me take a look.'

Jed quickly winked over Dennis's shoulder at Venus, who appeared at the side of the office. Then he gingerly took off his trainer and sock.

Venus saw Dennis crouching down and made her move. She knew the window of opportunity was tiny.

If Dennis discovered her, he'd go crazy. It had to be an in and out job. She watched him leaning over Jed and felt a twinge of guilt. But it only lasted a second. She rapidly crept up the steps at the side of the office.

The office was a rectangular room with a large desk at the far end, flanked on either side by a large grey filing cabinet. On the desk was a pad of paper, a pencil holder with several neatly sharpened pencils, a pad of

Post-it Notes and a black telephone. There was a blue office chair behind the desk.

Venus crossed the room towards the left filing cabinet. All four of its drawers were locked. She cursed silently and slid behind the chair. She could hear Jed and Dennis still talking outside.

The top three drawers of the other filing cabinet were also locked. But the fourth slid open. She rifled through a few files, all of which related to insurance matters connected to Riley Croft. Beyond the last of these was a bright orange folder, labelled 'Camp Applications'.

She pulled it out and took a quick peek out of the window. Dennis was helping Jed stand and getting him to put a bit of weight on his 'injured' foot. She had a minute – maybe two, max.

Inside the file was a set of completed application forms, and she quickly found Franco's. At the top were all his personal details. She grabbed a pencil, tore off a Post-it note and began to scribble furiously.

At the bottom of the page was Franco's personal statement setting out why he wanted to attend stunt camp. His writing was unusual – long and spindly. She read it quickly then checked outside. Her heart went into panic mode. Jed was limping away and Dennis was walking back to the office. Venus stuffed Franco's form back into the file, pushed the file back into its correct place and closed the cabinet.

She ran across the floor, hearing Dennis's footsteps crunching over the gravel towards the office. She had about ten seconds before he turned the corner and reached the office steps. She yanked open the door and leaped over the steps just managing to roll underneath the Portakabin office as Dennis's feet turned the corner and hit the bottom step.

Venus waited until Dennis has been inside for thirty seconds, then hurried away – dialling a number on her mobile as she went.

17.03

Venus met Jed at a cross in the pathways.

'Did you get what you wanted?' he asked, studying her face carefully with his light-blue eyes.

'No,' Venus replied, catching his gaze.

'What were you looking for?'

'It's really boring – just a family thing. But thanks for helping me out. You were brilliant.'

'Are you ever going to tell me?' Jed asked.

'Maybe, but I promise you it's nothing to get excited about.'

'OK.' He sighed. 'But don't forget, I'm always available for decoy work.'

Venus grinned.

'I'm heading back to the dorm,' Jed told her.

'See you later?'

'Definitely.'

20.05

Venus nodded hellos as she walked into the common room. She noticed something lying on top of a pile of books – a green ordnance survey map of the local area, which looked very familiar.

She plucked it out, sidled over to a deep blue armchair and sat down. She spread the map out on the low wooden table in front of her. It didn't take her long to locate Riley Croft and she traced her finger along the paper, locating the nearest stretch of coastline. It was called Travellers' Cove.

She was so engrossed in the map that she was late to detect the tread of footsteps. She looked up and saw Franco approaching. The back of a tatty brown armchair obscured his view of the low table. She quickly folded the map and stuffed it into her jacket pocket.

Franco slumped down into the armchair next to hers. 'What were you just looking at?' he asked.

Venus felt a shiver of unease snake down her spine. She shifted slightly in her seat. 'I wasn't looking at anything.'

'It looked like you were studying something.'

'I'm too tired to study anything.'

She leaned forward in the armchair and suddenly noticed out of the corner of her eye that the end of the map was sticking out of her jacket pocket. She quickly looked away hoping Franco hadn't seen it.

They sat in silence for a few seconds then Venus yawned, stretched and stood up, picking up her jacket in the same movement. There was a slight crinkling sound as the map brushed against her.

Franco looked up.

'I'm off to bed,' Venus said.

Franco mumbled something inaudible.

Venus walked towards the door, stuffing the map deeper into her jacket on the way.

20.33

The woman with silver eyes knocked briskly on a blue door bearing a sign proclaiming Night Fire Technology. A man with a thick beard opened the door and ushered her inside, his red-rimmed eyes nervously flicking back and forth down the empty corridor. She followed him along a dark passage to a large whitewashed room. Inside was another man, a small, spindly creature who stood against a wall – his eyes narrowly checking her out.

The only furniture in the room was a small circle of black office chairs. The bearded man indicated for the woman to sit down. They sat opposite each other while the spindly man remained standing.

'Is there a problem?' asked the bearded man.

'I'm used to deadlines being met,' she replied coldly.

The man smiled anxiously. 'This is only a minor setback,' he replied. 'I guarantee you'll get your order.'

'When?' she demanded.

'Possibly in the next few days,' he said, wringing his hands, 'more likely a week.'

She stared at him for a few seconds, her top lip curling upwards ever so slightly. Then she stood up. He offered his hand to shake.

She held out her hand in return.

But instead of shaking his, she suddenly lunged forward, grabbed him under the chin and slammed him against the wall, knocking his chair to the floor. Her face was millimetres away from his. His breath smelled of stale coffee and rust. Her grip was incredibly powerful and his face was reddening with the pressure being forced against his neck. She spun her head round and spotted the spindly man advancing towards her.

'Back off!' she shouted.

The bearded man nodded his head as best as he

could. 'Do what she says,' he uttered hoarsely. The spindly man halted.

She turned back to face the bearded man. 'This is the situation,' she hissed, her hand still grasping his throat. 'You deliver my order within the next forty-eight hours and you'll never see or hear from me again. Fail to do this and you'll receive a visit from some of my associates. Do you get it?'

The bearded man nodded fearfully, a thin trickle of sweat sliding down either side of his face. 'Perfectly clear,' he croaked, his breathing laboured and painful. 'I'll see to it straight away.'

She held him against the wall for another few seconds and then suddenly released him. He crumpled to the floor, clasping his throat and coughing. The spindly man rushed over to his side, scowling at her furiously.

'Forty-eight hours,' she repeated, walking back to the passage.

As the spindly man helped his colleague to his feet, they heard the door slamming shut behind her.

🏃 Chapter 13

22.32

'Venus, it's Kate. Can you talk?'

'Sure,' whispered Venus, pressing the mobile close to her ear in the darkened dorm.

'I might have been wrong about Franco.'

'What do you mean?'

'You know how I shouted at you when you phoned me earlier with that info from his application form?'

'Yes.'

'And the way I said you were crazy for sneaking into the site office?'

'Uh huh.'

'I think I need to apologise.'

'Why?'

'I went against my better judgement and indulged you, using my cousins' computer. And I reckon you're right to be suspicious.'

'Go on,' said Venus eagerly, feeling her heartbeat speeding up.

'Using that info you gave me, I got into his sixth-form college database – it was easy. I looked up his course details, attendance records, that sort of thing.'

'And?'

'Nothing. There's no record of him at all.'

'Maybe you missed something?' whispered Venus.

Kate tutted. 'No way. I checked every category twice and then cross-referenced them. The answer was always the same.'

'OK, he could have left that college. That would explain the lack of details.'

'Possibly, but then I checked the e-mail address and phone number he gave. They both drew blanks.'

'You're joking?'

'I'm not.'

'What about his home address?'

'The road mentioned on his form is a tiny cul-de-sac with seven houses. The consent form from his parents had the same address. There aren't any Danes living in that road. In fact there aren't any Danes living in that whole area of London.'

'No!'

'Yes!'

Venus pressed the phone closer to her ear. 'Are you sure about all of this, Kate?'

'A hundred percent.'

'So what does it mean?'

'It means,' Kate paused for a few seconds, 'that Franco Dane doesn't exist.'

DAY SIX

🏃 Chapter 14

21.27

Venus sat on her bed going over the events of the day. The morning's fitness work out had been gruelling. The afternoon's paint-balling game had been brilliant fun – with Donna, Cleo and Polly in a group up against Tariq, Carl and Rob – but there was one incident that freaked Venus out.

She'd been hiding behind a tree when a bullet of paint whooshed just past her ear smacking into a wall to her left. Spinning round, she caught a momentary glimpse of her attacker – running in the opposite direction.

It was Franco.

This would have been all right if it hadn't been for the fact that Franco was *on her side*. *Why does he seem to have it in for me?* she thought. And why was there no record of him in any of the places he'd listed on his application form? He was definitely up to something but, however desperately she racked her brains, she just couldn't work it out.

She'd kept an eye on him at supper and during the post-supper chill-out in the common room, but now she'd given up on Franco-watching. All of the other girls had crashed out apart from Donna, who was lying on her bunk, listening to her iPod, with heavy eyelids. Venus closed the curtain next to her bunk, just as a long shadow suddenly dipped into view on the veranda and then vanished.

Her body and mind were suddenly prodded from weariness. She jumped off her bunk, padded over to the door and peered outside. She hurried back to her bed and pulled on her trainers, jeans and jacket.

'What are you doing?' whispered Donna sleepily.

'Toilet trip,' replied Venus.

'OK, later,' mumbled Donna.

Venus stepped outside the dorm. Franco was about fifty yards away and she expected him to return to his laptop lair. But instead of turning towards the outhouse, he headed for the wood leading to the front of the site.

Venus had to make a split-second decision. Either she went back to bed or she followed him – very possibly on a cold, wild goose chase.

She tied up the laces on her trainers and went after him.

Franco entered the wooded enclave. Venus jogged silently along the path behind him, the trees looming over her. On the other side of the wood, she saw his outline stopping by the Riley Croft sign, before turning left on to the road. After a few steps, he looked over his shoulder. Venus quickly leaned back against a tree, the shadows immediately engulfing her.

She waited a few seconds and then crept out after him. She could see his dark shape moving briskly ahead. Pinning herself against the steep grass verge with its cornucopia of arching flowers and weeds, Venus trailed him down the road.

The nearest village was a good couple of miles away, but this seemed to be where he was heading. There was nothing else on the road in that direction – Venus remembered that from the van journey to the site. She stuck a good distance behind Franco, near enough to see him, but allowing herself enough space to duck completely out of sight if he turned around.

Half an hour later, he walked down the last stretch of the steep hill until it plateaued and the village loomed into view – its streetlamps giving off orbs of yellow light. Franco pressed on, past a couple of thatched cottages and headed for the entrance of the local pub, the Bear and Fox. He pulled open the door and disappeared inside.

Venus stopped for a second. Maybe he was just a drinker. Alcohol wasn't allowed on site. He could easily pass for eighteen and he'd have no problems getting served. Venus chewed her bottom lip. Back to the site or keep on his trail?

The sounds of chatting and laughter briefly spilled out on to the street, as a man lurched out of the pub and staggered down the road in the opposite direction. The noise disappeared again as the heavy pub door shut behind him.

Venus pulled her jacket tighter and crept forward.

22.10

Gail searched the kitchen drawers. She was sure she'd recently seen some glue in one of them. One of the partners at her law firm had a son who was going to be five next week and Gail wanted to make a card for him. She wasn't the most artistic person in the world, but she enjoyed being a bit creative. Maybe she'd just have to nip down to the shops tomorrow.

Then a thought struck her. She had a vague memory that she'd seen a pot of ancient glue elsewhere in the house. She went upstairs and entered her daughter's bedroom. She pulled open Venus's cupboard.

At the front, there was a mound of art stuff – paint pots, brushes, pads, pencil tins – Venus was a great hoarder. Gail pulled out a large box of ancient crayons and pushed a tin of pencils to one side. Behind a sketchpad was a tub of glue. It would do. As she was reaching for the tub, something else caught her eye.

It was a photograph, whose edge was just jutting out from beneath an old cereal packet. She reached out and pulled the photo towards her.

It was black and white.

As soon as she recognised it, a chill slithered down her spine.

Chapter 15

22.14

Venus tiptoed forward, crouched down and scampered over to one of the pub's windows. She raised her head slowly and looked inside. The bar room was pretty busy and she scanned the room, expecting to see Franco ordering a drink or sitting down on a bar stool.

But he wasn't there.

She checked again, slowly eyeing all corners of the bar. OK, maybe he went to the toilet first. She waited a couple of minutes, but he still didn't appear.

As she crouched down again, the door suddenly swung open and a couple of young women fell out, laughing noisily as they set off down the road. Just before the door swung shut, Venus spotted the opening to a passageway inside, with a sign above the entrance stating, *Restaurant – this way*.

She moved along the side of the pub and around the back. Peering through a low window, she saw a series of round tables. The restaurant room was empty.

Venus cursed. Where was he? He couldn't have just vanished.

She took a step back and looked up. A small pool of light shone out of a window on the third floor. She studied the wall thoughtfully.

A minute later, she was halfway up the side of the building, the plastic black drainpipe wobbling slightly as it supported her weight.

Venus was an expert climber.

Her best climb had been scaling the enormous façade of Cleopatra's Palace on the set of *The Scales of the Pharaoh*. She'd worn a harness under her jacket, but it still felt incredibly dangerous and exciting. And reaching the plinth on the top was pure elation. She'd also done the less glamorous but equally useful ten week rock-climbing course at the local leisure centre.

So it didn't take long for her to get her head level

with the bottom of the third-floor windowsill. She moved up a few inches more and peered inside, her feet resting on a horizontal length of drainpipe. Luckily, one of the heavy brown drapes was slightly open and this gave Venus a good view of the room. In one corner was a round blue table, with a couple of empty beer glasses on its surface. Next to the table, on the floor, was a wooden chest with seashells embedded in its surface.

There were two people inside, sitting at the table, talking. One of them was Franco.

A jutting-out section of wall obscured her view of the other person's face, but she was sure it was a middle-aged man. All she could see was his left arm, which was adorned with a sprawling and intricate tattoo, depicting a boat and an island, and some very fine lettering. It looked like the one Venus had recently seen across the back of some Z-list ex-sailor celebrity on TV.

Franco's friend must have some sort of naval connection, Venus thought, as she noted the silver and black snake ring on his index finger.

Venus shivered, clung to the windowsill and watched. The two of them were talking in very low voices and she couldn't hear anything. Franco looked far more animated than he ever did at camp. He was nodding earnestly as the navy man spoke to him. A moment later the man placed a black case on the table, rolled the combination lock and flicked it open. His tattooed arm withdrew a thin metal tube marked at the top with a dark-green cross. He handed it to Franco. There was another symbol on the lower half, but Franco placed the tube very carefully inside his inner jacket pocket, denying Venus an accurate look.

The man reached into the briefcase again and produced a single sheet of paper. Franco studied it very carefully, closing his eyes several times and moving his lips, as if he was trying to memorise what he saw. When he'd finished, he tore it into tiny scraps. As these fell on to the table, the man picked them up and stuffed them all into his outer jacket pocket.

Venus stared with fascination at the scene inside the room. *What was in the metal tube? Why had Franco ripped the sheet of paper? Who was the naval guy?* As these questions flashed through her mind, the drainpipe on which she was standing suddenly wobbled dramatically. In a split second she lost her footing and her grip on the windowsill. She lurched sharply to the left.

She reached out to grab the sill again, but it was too late.

A second later she fell backwards through the air.

🏃 Chapter 16

22.26

Dennis locked up the site office and sat down on the wooden steps outside. He took a deep lungful of country air and smiled. He'd fallen in love with this part of Devonshire on his first visit with Doreen years ago. In his more dreamy moments he thought about buying a cottage and retiring down here.

But he knew that day was a long way off. He'd miss the buzz of the city too much. Besides he was nowhere near ready to give up his career as a stunt artist and coordinator.

His smile vanished though when he remembered the light blue envelope nestling in his jacket pocket. He'd received it a couple of days before camp, but he hadn't opened it yet. Maybe he should have got rid of it and pretended it had never reached him? It was a comforting thought, but he knew it wasn't an option.

He *had* to open it some time.

He took it out and prepared to slide his finger under the flap. But he didn't get the chance because a flicker of light further down the path interrupted him. He quickly lifted his torch and stood up, squashing the envelope back inside his jacket.

His boots crunched over the ground as he hurried over to see what was going on.

22.27

'What was that?' It was Franco's voice.

The third-floor window flung open.

'I'm sure I heard something,' Franco snapped, gazing out at the purplish-black night sky.

As Venus had fallen she'd desperately reached out and caught on to the bottom of a hanging flower basket. Luckily for her, the basket was firmly secured to the wall with metal chains and, as she was underneath it, she was undetectable to Franco. But she was only about five metres below him.

The only problem was that Venus was dangling outside a second-floor window and a portly woman had just entered the room, carrying a large bundle of laundry. The ground was quite a distance below and however well she cushioned her fall, Venus knew she'd be lucky to escape without injury, particularly to her knees, which would take the brunt of her fall.

Why did I get myself into this mess? She groaned inwardly.

One look outside and the laundry woman would spot an unidentified flying teenager and probably call the police.

Venus held on with all of her strength as the woman picked up a long green dress and turned her head towards the window. If she moved a tiny bit further round she'd definitely see Venus. But at that second, a phone rang on a bedside table and the woman went over to answer it.

Venus steadied herself and stretched her right foot out to the window ledge. She put all of her strength on to her foot and pulled herself on to the sill. Moving stealthily, she scaled back up the wall to the third floor, clung to the window ledge and listened. There was now no sound coming from inside. Gradually she pulled herself further up, until her eyes were parallel with the bottom of the window frame. She looked in to the room.

It was empty.

She reached out and pressed her hand against the window. Franco had shut it but not locked it. She pushed it open and eased herself inside. She checked the table and chairs. Nothing. She got down on her knees and started to inspect the carpet. At first, it seemed completely bare, but then she spotted it.

At the base of the chair on which Franco had been sitting a few minutes ago, was a tiny scrap of paper. It must have slipped through his hands when he was tearing the sheet. She reached down and picked it up.

Written in pencil was *n20*. Venus held the scrap. What did *n20* mean? Was it some sort of code? She looked at her watch – she needed to get back to the site

Venus didn't want to risk the wall and the laundry woman again, so she opened the door and found herself at the top of a narrow flight of stairs. She hurried down, turned right and stepped through a black doorway. She found herself by the side of the pub, next to a couple of large rubbish bins. She dialled Kate's number on her mobile.

23.01

There was no sign of Franco on the way back. Venus walked past the wooden Riley Croft site entrance and crept swiftly along the path through the trees. She was just stepping out of the wooded enclave when a light suddenly came on and blinded her.

'Who's that?' she demanded, shielding her eyes.

'It's me.'

Venus relaxed. It was Dennis.

The torchlight sunk and she saw him silhouetted in the darkness.

'Granddad,' she said, trying to sound cool, 'what are you doing here?'

'I saw Angie stumbling around in the darkness. She was just going to the toilet, so I guided her there. But when I looked in at the girls' dorm, your bunk was empty. I checked everywhere and couldn't find you. Where the hell have you been?'

Venus guiltily slipped into 'lie' mode. 'I couldn't sleep so I went for a walk to get some fresh night air.'

'Why didn't you walk round here? You know you're not allowed off site.'

'I know, Granddad, sorry. It was a stupid thing to do.'

'It was more than stupid, Venus.'

'You're right. I won't do it again.'

Dennis gazed at her questioningly for a few seconds and then squeezed her shoulder. 'OK, Venus, but if you can't sleep again, come and get me. Don't leave the site.'

'Will do,' she said, smiling.

Dennis was about to reply when a rustling sound echoed behind them. Venus spun round, looking for any sign of movement. What if Franco had seen her hanging beneath the flower basket? Maybe he was now spying on *her*? Dennis shone his torch but the ray of light only picked out the gnarled branches and silvery bark of the trees.

'Come on,' said Dennis. 'I'll walk you back to the dorm.'

DAY SEVEN

🏃Chapter 17

07.46

The first rays of the morning sun filtered under the dorm curtains and nudged Venus awake. For a minute she couldn't remember where she was. She rubbed her eyes and then it all came back to her: Franco's pub rendezvous; the thin metal tube; the guy with the naval tattoo.

She lay in bed, going over everything. Franco was definitely involved in something dodgy, but what? Venus tried to put all of the pieces of the jigsaw together, but she couldn't connect them. After fifteen minutes her brain felt weary from all of its efforts and she was about to switch off, when a thought suddenly crept into her head. Maybe there was a link between all of them.

Venus sat up quickly.

Yes, she could see it now. Franco could be caught up

in some sort of drug-smuggling racket. She'd once seen a TV programme about it, though she hadn't paid much attention because there weren't any stunts to watch. She wondered if the metal tube she'd seen could have contained some kind of drug. Franco might be going to make a 'drop' somewhere along the coastline – possibly at the Travellers' Cove she'd spotted on the map? That could be why he'd been studying stretches of water on his laptop – and why he'd met someone with naval connections. Venus vaguely remembered reading somewhere that loads of drugs were still shipped in and out of the country. It all suddenly seemed to fit together – apart from $n20$, which still remained a complete mystery to her.

Venus stayed in bed, working on her new theory and getting more certain by the minute that she'd stumbled upon the truth. She agonised over whether she should talk to Dennis. She so wanted to and yet it still seemed too risky. It would be so humiliating if he didn't take her seriously. Or if she was wrong.

20.15

The Franco situation was at the front of Venus's mind all day. After supper she sat with loads of people on the floor of the boys' dorm, laughing about the day's events, especially the steep climb down a treacherous waterfall. Greg was asleep on his bottom bunk and snoring loudly. Franco was lying on his top bunk, reading a book. Tariq was sitting by the door, half-listening to his iPod.

'When that massive branch fell on Spike I thought he was going to get knocked out!' said Polly, winking at Spike.

'I nearly got killed because you didn't move quickly enough,' Spike responded.

'It was like that scene in *Desert Traps*,' said Venus, keeping one eye on Franco. 'You know the bit where Brad Fraser's double swings from the underside of that bridge.'

'That was a wicked stunt!' called Tariq.

They were interrupted by the sound of Dennis's voice, cutting through the dorm chat. 'Venus, can I have a quick word with you in the site office?'

Venus stood up reluctantly, her eyes flitting over to Franco's bunk. 'What is it, Granddad?' she asked, looking back at the dorm as she walked.

'I'll show you in a second,' he replied.

They reached the office. She waited as he unlocked the padlock and they went inside. Dennis flicked on the light. He reached under his desk, pulled open a drawer and held up a slim silver necklace.

'It's for your mum's birthday. What d'you reckon?'

'She'll love it.' Venus nodded, already edging back towards the door.

'Everything OK, Venus? You seem a bit jittery.'

'I'm cool, Granddad. I was just in the middle of a great conversation.'

'Of course, off you go,' he said with an apologetic smile.

She gave him a quick hug and ran back to the dorm.

The big group were still on the floor chatting. Greg was still snoring. Tariq was nodding along to his music. But Franco was nowhere to be seen.

21.34

Gail turned the black and white photo over with her thumb and forefinger for the umpteenth time that day. Did Venus know it was in her cupboard? Or was it just another scrap of paper amongst all of the other mess. If she did know about it, how long had she had it? And why hadn't she asked Gail any questions about it? Gail had spent so long trying to forget about Elliot and the photo unsettled her. She stared at it, remembering the exact second it was taken.

The past was intruding on the present.

She shivered as a catalogue of memories came flooding back.

The blue van inched down the tarmac lane and around the corner, easing itself into the large yard at the back of the retail park. The silver-eyed woman applied the brake. She got out, climbed the small flight of stone steps and knocked twice on shutter number thirteen.

Almost immediately a humming noise sounded and the shutter began to move up, its metal lines shimmying in the moonlight like crocodile scales. A small man with wispy hair and a squint appeared behind the shutter. He glanced at her nervously for a few seconds and then headed back inside and out of sight. A minute later, he reappeared, pushing a trolley with a large metallic item – a couple of metres long and half a metre wide, resembling a small section of tree trunk – resting on its surface.

The woman opened the van's back doors. The man hurriedly slid the item across onto its floor. His face was glistening with perspiration. The woman closed the doors. She reached inside her jacket, pulled out a brown envelope and handed it to the man. He grunted with satisfaction and hurried back inside. She climbed back into the van as shutter thirteen lowered behind her.

Turning the ignition, she pulled the van slowly back on to the tarmac drive. She was fifty metres from the exit when two security guards appeared out of the darkness. They had dogs.

'Stop the van,' one of the guards shouted.

Instantly she hit the accelerator.

'It's coming at us!' the other guard yelled.

The van lunged forward and the guards just managed to pull their baying dogs out of its path.

'I've got the plate number!' shouted the first guard over the howling of the dogs.

The silver-eyed woman drove for a couple of miles before stopping in a lay-by. She changed the van's front and back number plates. It was only a few seconds work.

Then she was on the move again.

DAY EIGHT

🏃 Chapter 18

08.40

The next morning rain lashed against the buildings dotted across Riley Croft. As people were finishing their toast and cereal, Dennis stood up.

'I've had a call from Alan Docker,' he announced. 'Unfortunately the horse riding today is off.'

There was a collective groan.

Venus was gutted. She'd only ever ridden for half an hour on the shoot for *The Power of the Wind*. And, even then, it was a small pony, not a horse. But it barely distracted her from thinking about Franco.

Franco had been away the night before for just over an hour. Venus was confused. If he'd been intending to get to the beach and back he could never have done it in that time. So where on earth had he gone? If it *was* drugs, had he delivered or collected them yet?

'Unfortunately, Sampson – one of Alan Docker's

horses we'd be using – has taken ill,' Dennis continued, 'and Alan's worried about the other horses picking something up too. So he wants to rest them today.' Dennis looked at the disappointed faces around him. 'I know it's a downer,' he said, 'but I'll make sure we get in a good horse session before camp ends.'

There were mumbles and nods from people.

'That means,' said Dennis, grinning fiendishly, 'we've got a spare session. I'm in the mood for a waterlogged assault course. The rain will make it even more treacherous than usual.'

13.30

The assault course had been a drenched frenzy. Narinder got so much water in her ears that she couldn't hear anything for fifteen minutes, and Polly fell in the mud four times. Showered and fed, everyone now stood facing Dennis in a clearing between the trees. The rain had stopped and the sun was just emerging from behind an ash-grey cloud.

'This little beauty is called a foil,' Dennis announced.

Sixteen pairs of eyes focused on the thin metal sword he picked up from a wooden box on the ground.

'You'll have seen foils in loads of films,' Dennis continued. 'The sword fight in *Witch Legend* is a good example.'

Venus knew the film well. Kelly Tanner stood in for Saffron Richie in a classic sword fight on the roof of Buckingham Palace.

'Foils are very flexible,' Dennis explained, bending the sword towards him. 'They're also the smallest sword in the trade. So, if any of you were hoping for a King Arthur moment, forget it. The épées and sabres can wait. The foil has a rounded tip at its end to avoid injury. However, foils can be dangerous if they're misused, and accidents do happen, so be careful.'

Venus felt a shot of excitement as Dennis reached down to get the rest of the foils from the box. Like everyone else, she'd had very little experience of sword work and was totally up for it.

'OK,' said Dennis, nodding. 'First I want to get you all used to holding the foils. When everyone feels comfortable with their grip, we'll try a few simple moves.'

'Good work,' Dennis announced ten minutes later, having weaved between people, altering a grip here, straightening a back there. 'Now we're going to do a very simple sequence in pairs. Cleo, come here a second.'

Cleo stepped forward, clutching her foil.

'The first person, who we'll call the "attacker", will jab left,' Dennis explained, demonstrating the action in slow motion. 'They'll be blocked by the second person the "defender", that's you, Cleo.'

He pulled her foil towards him, showing the arc of the block.

'Following this, the attacker will tap the defender's left shoulder.' He did this carefully. 'OK, Cleo?'

She nodded and they went through the sequence again, only this time a bit faster.

'Excellent.' Dennis nodded. 'Three moves. Here are your partners.'

He quickly split everyone into pairs. 'Keep on until I call out and then the attacker becomes the defender and vice versa.'

Venus was paired first with Polly and then Greg. After a while she began to feel more confident handling her sword.

Dennis set a range of other increasingly complex sequences. The final one consisted of nine foil strokes and involved fighting on the move.

'I want you to spread out much more this time,' Dennis explained. 'Get the feel of combining motion with sword-handling.'

Dennis indicated for Venus to pair up with Franco. Venus felt her chest tighten, but there was no trace of any negative emotion on Franco's face. He seemed completely nonplussed.

'Shall I be the attacker first?' Venus asked, still being very wary of him.

'Whatever,' said Franco with a shrug.

Venus straightened up and held her sword upright, ready to begin. Franco followed suit. Venus cut forward.

By her fifth turn as the attacker they were both moving pretty fluidly. Venus was pushing forward, Franco inching backwards in defence like Dennis had instructed.

After they changed roles, it took Venus a while to get used to the stepping backwards, but after three goes she was beginning to feel quietly pleased with herself.

On the fourth go, Franco was due to end the sequence by pushing Venus's foil aside, but as Venus began to relax, his foil suddenly came crashing down towards her face. She was totally off her guard. His foil whipped through the air and caught her on the cheek. Its edge bit into her skin and she winced as a searing bolt of pain flashed across her face.

'*What are you doing?*' she asked in shock, grasping her cheek.

'Sorry,' muttered Franco, 'Dennis was right about accidents.'

'That *wasn't* an accident,' Venus hissed.

'What do you mean?' Franco suddenly looked very aggressive.

Something in Venus suddenly snapped. He *must* know she was shadowing him and this was his way of warning her to back off. Well, she wasn't frightened of him.

Without hesitation, she gripped her foil and swung it towards Franco's face.

He blocked her stroke. 'What are *you* doing?' He spat out the words.

Venus pulled her foil away and went for a jab against his stomach. But he was equal to it and blocked her again. Venus's temper was boiling over. She quickly checked behind her. The rest of the group were scattered over a wide area and Dennis was a long way away.

'You're crazy,' Franco snarled. He pushed off from a tree and went on the offensive. Venus found herself back-stepping, blocking blows that rained down towards her.

When his foil came down again, Venus was waiting for him. Her sword smashed against his. She equalled him for skill, and they both held their ground, their foils pressing against each other, their faces nearly touching, both desperately attempting to push the other backwards.

Venus suddenly pulled back to give Franco a sense she was weakening. He took the bait and moved forward sensing victory, but was taken by complete surprise when she lunged and knocked him backwards. As he fell, she high-kicked the foil out of his hand. He toppled onto the ground as the foil flew over his head.

'I guess Dennis was right about accidents,' spat Venus.

Franco stood up and stomped over to retrieve his sword, which was lying beside a gorse bush. Venus's cheek burned with pain. But she wasn't going to let Franco see her discomfort.

'And stop there!' called Dennis. 'All foils back to me now.'

Venus glared at Franco as she walked off towards the others and threw her sword into the box. Dennis caught her elbow and swung her round to face him.

'How did you pick that up?' he asked, pointing to the cut on her cheek.

'I fell,' she explained, 'against a tree . . . scratched myself.'

'Doesn't look like a scratch,' Dennis said with a questioning stare. He looked at Franco, who was sulkily returning his sword to the box. 'Does it hurt? Do you need first aid?'

'It's nothing,' Venus replied.

Dennis let go of her. She was about to walk off when she spotted Franco staring at her furiously.

Venus knew that things with him had changed for ever.

They were enemies now.

🏃 Chapter 19

16.45

'What's up, Venus? You've got your worried voice on.'

'I'm fine, Mum, really.'

Venus was sitting on the steps at the back of the canteen.

'Come on, Venus. Tell me, what's up?'

'It's nothing . . . I . . . I just had a bit of a falling out with one of the boys here – a guy called Franco.' The minute the words left her mouth Venus regretted them.

'What sort of falling out?' Gail demanded anxiously.

Venus responded quickly. 'He was just being a bit of a pain.'

'Well, what was it about?'

'Honestly, Mum, it's cool – it was just a misunderstanding.'

'Have you talked to Dennis about it?'

'There's no need to involve Dennis. It was over in five seconds.'

'Well why did you mention it? It must be bothering you.'

'Leave it, Mum. It's no big deal. I promise you.'

Gail hesitated. 'OK, Venus. But make sure you sort it out. And if you can't, let Granddad sort it out. That's what he's there for.'

'Course I will, Mum.'

'Good, now what about the food?'

'I've told you – it's fine,' Venus replied.

'What have they been feeding you then?'

She began going over the day's menus, but kept feeling her cheek. It stung like crazy.

20.31

After supper, Dennis managed to find a dry patch of land in a sheltered part of the site, and Donna and Spike helped to build a fire. Dennis's legendary Night Activity would be starting soon.

Venus dug deeply into the warm pockets of her fleece, and sat on a log in front of the fire, a little apart from the others who were talking and laughing. She had made some strong friendships in the past week, but tonight for the first time she felt alone.

Her cheek still ached even though she'd put some of Polly's sting cream on it. She tried not to think about it or about the look in Franco's eyes. Maybe she should just confront him in front of the others and Dennis? Ask him about the pub meeting, the coastline and everything else? Everyone had been concerned about her injury, but no one suspected Franco of foul play. Venus didn't think it was a good idea to arouse suspicion yet.

She stared into the yellows, blues and oranges of the fire. Someone sat down next to her and she looked up.

'Jed,' she started.

'I saw you kick the sword out of Franco's hand,' he said quietly.

Venus froze – she'd been certain no one had witnessed any of the sword fight.

'We were just messing about,' she lied.

'It didn't look like messing about,' Jed answered. 'You both seemed well steamed up.'

Venus didn't say anything.

'It was a lie about scratching your face on a tree, wasn't it? He did it.'

Venus nodded slowly.

'Has this got anything to do with you sneaking into the office?' asked Jed, looking at her with big concerned eyes.

Venus took a deep breath. 'We just got a bit carried away with the foils and the office thing, well that's –'

'What's going on, Venus? You can trust me.'

Venus ached to tell Jed the truth, but things were already complicated enough.

'I know I can trust you,' she said with a smile, 'I just . . . can't talk about it.'

Jed squinted at her with uncertainty. He was about to say something else, but he reluctantly accepted that this particular conversation was over.

'OK,' he said, managing a half smile at her.

But it didn't feel OK.

Venus turned back to the flames and kicked a stray strip of sparks back into the fire.

🏃 Chapter 20

21.26

'Everyone know what they're doing?'

The three other faces nodded.

'Good,' replied Venus. 'Let's win it.'

After Dennis had put out the fire, he'd told people to go to their dorms to get ready. He'd then split them into four teams of four. Venus was put with Donna, Polly and Spike. Each team was assigned a 'base' at different points around the site. These bases were a good distance away from each other. The team's first job was to make a base shelter out of anything they could find in the woods. Venus's team had done this and it was now almost totally pitch black.

Each team had been allocated ten colour-coded pegs to keep in their base – Venus's team's were red. The idea of the game was to hold on to as many of the pegs as possible while stealing as many of the other team's pegs. The team with the most pegs at the end of the game were the winners. The team with fewest pegs would be on washing-up duty for the rest of the week. This was a big enough incentive to get everybody motivated.

The red team had unanimously appointed Venus as their leader.

'OK,' Venus continued, 'Spike and I will attack the other bases first. In twenty minutes we'll switch. Unless anything radical happens, let's carry on like that until we win this game.'

Venus's plan worked well and as the game neared to a close, the reds had lost just three of their pegs while collecting twelve from the other teams. They had to be in the lead.

'I'm just going to check out the blue team again,' Venus whispered to Spike. 'See you in a minute.'

Venus quickly checked around her. She could hear cries in the distance, some of victory, others of defeat. She trotted on to the path and walked quickly towards the boys' dorm. The door creaked open and she looked in. The room was bathed in moonlight. It smelled dankly of wet clothes and mulched up leaves. She hesitated for a second. *Perhaps this wasn't such a great idea.* She could easily go straight back to the red base.

She pushed the door further open and stepped inside – looking behind her to check that no one else was around. Reaching Franco's bunk she saw his green bag on the floor. She knelt down and unzipped it. There had to be some more clues somewhere.

She pulled out a pair of jeans, a sweatshirt, a tatty novel and a pack of chewing gum before her hand came into contact with the cool casing of a mobile phone. Pulling it out quickly, she turned it on. Someone screamed outside. She had to be quick – the night activity only had a couple of minutes left.

The phone flickered into life with a tinny jingle. Venus selected 'Messages' and then 'Inbox'. Footsteps approached outside. Venus held her breath. They stopped for a second and then hurried past the door.

She highlighted the most recent message. It had been sent at four p.m. that afternoon.

It appeared on the screen. 3205.

That was it. Four digits. 3205.

She pressed the 'Return Call' option, but the phone bleeped twice, and the message 'NO PHONE NUMBER' appeared. If it wasn't a phone number, what was it? Venus groaned as she thought of all the possibilities. She was just about to open the previous text message when she heard the door handle turning.

'What are you doing in here?' asked Franco, turning the lights on and appearing in the doorway.

'I'm looking for a torch.'

Venus was kneeling by Jed's bed. She glanced across at Franco's bag. She'd got everything back in it, but hadn't managed to close the zip completely. It was the first time she'd been alone with Franco since the sword fight.

'Well, where is it?' he asked accusingly, looking at her empty hands. 'The game's almost over.'

'Must be somewhere else,' Venus replied, standing up.

Franco stood where he was, glaring at her. 'If I was found snooping around in the girls' dorm, I'd never hear the last of it,' he said icily.

'Not if you were there for a torch,' Venus answered, eyeing the door and staring back at him.

The boom of Dennis's voice sounded somewhere outside.

'Looks like the game's over,' noted Venus, walking towards him.

For a few seconds Franco stood blocking her way with his arm resting across the door. He stared at her suspiciously and it looked as if he was going to say something else, but his mouth stayed closed.

Venus moved his arm out of her way and walked out into the darkness – towards the deep sound of Dennis's voice.

🏃 Chapter 21

22.45

The night activity was long over when Venus heard low voices on the path ahead of her. It was Dennis and Alan. She crept closer to listen, hiding in the shadows so that Dennis wouldn't see her. She was out well beyond his nightly curfew.

'Sampson's not too good,' Alan was saying. 'The vet isn't quite sure what it is. He's prescribed antibiotics, but thinks it might be a virus. That horse is normally a thirsty beast – he's always at the trough outside his barn, but at the minute he won't go near it. And to make matters worse, two of my best milking cows are looking rough tonight – lethargic, unhappy – not themselves.'

'Sorry to hear that,' Dennis replied.

'Could just be a bout of seasonal flu. I just hope none of the others get it. I've isolated them in one of the small barns, well away from the rest of the animals. Hopefully they'll be fine in a couple of days.'

Venus stood for a few seconds as their conversation turned to the weather. She hurried back down the path, stopping at the boys' dorm door and poking her head inside.

'Hey, Venus,' called Jed, who was lying on his top bunk, flicking through a football magazine.

'Hi,' she replied distractedly, as something by Franco's bed suddenly caught her eye. A pair of his wet combats was drying on a dorm radiator alongside jeans and track pants. But the watermark on Franco's combats was much higher than on anybody else's trousers.

Seeing this stirred something in the back of Venus's mind.

'What's up?' Jed asked, noticing her puzzled expression, 'Are you coming in?'

'I'll catch you later,' she said quickly.

As Venus walked away from the boys' dorm, her sense of unease and foreboding increased with every step.

23.17

Dennis sat inside his campervan and locked the door. He flicked on the driver's light and pulled the light blue envelope from his pocket. He'd waited long enough – now was the time to open it. He held it still for a few seconds and then ripped open the envelope.

He pulled out the single sheet of white paper. It bore the usual address and had been typed in the familiar font. There were seven lines of text and Dennis read these quickly, realising at once that it was even worse news than he'd expected. A look of concern sprung across his face and he felt his fists clenching with tension.

He read it another couple of times and then replaced it in the envelope. It would need a response, but a written reply wouldn't suffice – he needed to act on it.

And by the look of things he didn't have much time.

23.45

Venus ran across the grass to the site classroom. The door was unlocked. She forced herself not to dwell too much on what she was doing. She just had to get on with it, however frightening and dangerous it seemed.

The moonlight filtered in through the blinds. There were four large tables in the classroom and a long workbench along the right wall. Above the workbench were two wide shelves containing a series of rectangular, plastic storage boxes. Each box was labelled and stored different pieces of geography and field study equipment. Venus walked slowly along the workbench, reading each label carefully. She stopped midway and pulled a box down.

Rifling through it she stopped with satisfaction and slipped a couple of items into her jacket pocket. A distant siren sounded as she stepped out of the classroom, but it barely registered.

Her mind was on the job ahead.

DAY NINE

🏃 Chapter 22

07.46

Venus silently pulled on a T-shirt, mud-splattered track pants and trainers. She'd asked Dennis last night if she could go for a short run off-site in the morning to warm up her body, and he'd said yes, but only for half an hour. Luckily no one else suggested joining in.

Venus ran along the path, through the trees and out on to the road. Turning right she quickly got into her stride. The early morning sun shone through the evaporating mist and as Venus ran she thought about confiding in Dennis. Was it time to tell him? Or should she still keep it all to herself? She just couldn't make up her mind. Her thinking was halted when she rounded the second corner in the road.

A hundred metres or so in the distance was a large windowless, metallic grey van parked right in front of

Docker's farm. The van had a satellite dish protruding from its roof. Three people in white biohazard outfits were unloading equipment from the back of the vehicle. Venus edged forward. A large sign had been erected outside the farm's front gate: STRICTLY NO ENTRY – AUTHORISED PERSONNEL ONLY.

One of the people in the white suits looked up and noticed Venus and started to walk towards her. Through the mask Venus could see a woman's face. She was wearing small round glasses and had thin lips.

'Who are you?' the woman asked, her voice muffled by the material covering her face.

'I'm staying at Riley Croft,' Venus replied.

The woman checked a sheet of paper. 'Dennis Spring is running a camp there?'

'Yes, he's my granddad.'

'OK.' The woman nodded. 'Someone will come down later to check all of the fences. Perhaps you could tell Mr Spring what's going on – though word's going to get round at any rate soon.'

Venus looked blank.

'Unfortunately there's been an outbreak of a rare flu at Docker's farm and we need to establish pretty quickly what caused it. So far a horse and two cows have been infected.'

Venus immediately thought of Sampson and the

two cows Alan had mentioned to Dennis on the path last night.

'The farm will be totally out of bounds,' the woman went on, 'it's a . . . very serious situation.' The woman then looked at Venus as if she was weighing up how much to say. 'It will all be on this morning's news,' said the woman, as much to herself as to Venus. 'It's the first case where a disease of this kind has spread to a human.'

Venus's mouth fell open.

'The farmer's daughter, Annie, was rushed to hospital last night,' the woman said, 'it's extremely serious.'

Venus remembered the siren she'd heard when she was leaving the site classroom the night before. 'Is she going to be OK?' she asked anxiously.

The woman's silence was ominous.

Annie could die.

'What about the animals?'

'They'll have to be destroyed.'

'All of them?'

'I'm afraid so. If the disease spreads beyond the farm there could be thousands, possibly tens of thousands of animal deaths and in terms of humans . . .'

The words clung to the air.

Venus stood silently trying to take this news in.

'We're confident though that we can contain the disease,' added the woman.

But as the woman was speaking, Venus's mind began to race and a look of horror covered her face. Could this be connected in some way to Franco? Maybe the drugs theory was wrong . . . What *was* in that tube?

'Are you OK?' asked the woman.

Venus managed a nod before turning and running back in the direction of the site.

🏃 Chapter 23

08.11

'Kate?' Venus spoke into her mobile as she walked back up the narrow track leading to Riley Croft. 'I've just been at the farm next door.'

Ten minutes later, having heard Venus's theory, Kate's tone became very serious. 'If you're right,' she said, 'and Franco is caught up in this disease situation, then things have got far too dangerous. You've got to tell Dennis and phone the police.'

'*No way*,' hissed Venus. 'Dennis would say he should never have introduced me to the stunt world –

that it's caused my imagination to go into overdrive.'

'Are you mad, Venus?' There was urgency in Kate's voice. 'You can't deal with this yourself.'

'I'll be extra careful,' Venus replied.

'It doesn't matter how careful you are, Venus. You're well out of your depth. Tell someone, and walk away from it.'

'OK. I'll leave it for a bit. But I'm not telling Dennis – at least not yet. And I'm certainly not alerting the police. I'll check out Franco's next move.'

'Please don't do *anything* crazy,' Kate pleaded.

'I'm not going to do anything, Kate. I'm just going to watch, OK?'

Kate sighed heavily. 'OK, Venus,' she conceded, 'but stay well back.'

When Venus returned to the site, she told Dennis exactly what she'd seen. He immediately phoned the farm, but there was no reply.

'I need to get the mountain bike trail started, but I'll keep trying Alan on my mobile,' Dennis said.

14.54

When the group returned mid-afternoon from the bike ride, the bio-suited woman Venus had seen earlier at Docker's farm was waiting for them. Dressed now in a business suit, she'd checked Riley Croft's fencing and was satisfied. She told Dennis and the group that no one except for strictly authorised personnel could now enter or leave Docker's farm. A team of armed police officers had been drafted in to make sure this rule was obeyed.

A little later, Dennis finally managed to get hold of Alan. Dennis looked ashen-faced as he listened to the news. Annie's condition was bad. And it was worsening by the hour.

18.33

The talk for the rest of the day was all about the disease. There had been an update on the local news just before supper – Cleo said she hoped it wouldn't make the national press, or they'd have everyone's parents rushing down to Riley Croft to take their children to safety. Some people in the group thought it must have been carried over from another part of the country; others said it might have been caused by pollution created in factories. Franco, however, sat back and said nothing.

Just before supper, Venus was troubled by another worry. Her phone was missing. She'd last seen it in the dorm before lunch. Jed helped her search the canteen, the common room and both dorms, but with no luck. They were just considering their next move when they heard footsteps on the path behind them. It was Franco.

'Found your phone?' he asked.

'Not yet,' Venus replied.

'Must be a real pain,' Franco said coolly.

Venus didn't like his tone. 'Back off, Franco,' she muttered crossly.

'What's up with her?' asked Franco looking innocently at Jed.

Venus suddenly snapped. 'I know all about you, *Franco Dane,*'

Franco looked shocked for a second. 'Really?' he replied. There was now anger in his voice, like when he'd attacked Venus with the foil.

Venus instinctively squared up to him, but Jed quickly stood between them.

'Leave it, Franco,' Jed said.

'Whatever,' Franco hissed as he brushed past them with a glare.

'I can't believe you just did that,' snapped Venus.

Jed looked taken aback. 'What do you mean?'

'I don't need you to fight my battles for me.'

'Hey Venus, I was only trying to be –'

'Well, don't bother!'

Venus stormed off, leaving Jed standing bemused in the middle of the pathway.

🏃 Chapter 24

19.22

The silver-eyed woman pulled the van to a halt and killed the engine. As the hum of the motor disappeared, she sat for a few seconds in the silence. Admittedly, it had been a little complicated to secure the goods, but all that mattered now was the end product. She'd never doubted her own abilities to pull this thing off – not for one second.

She climbed down, went round to the back of the van and pulled opened the doors. Her package lay there silently waiting for her command. She reached inside and clutched its end. She'd done all of the legwork in getting the package here.

Now it would finish the job for her.

21.26

Venus had noted the position of every police officer spread out around the Docker's farm perimeter fence. Ironically it was the front of the farm that offered her the best chance of entry without detection. The officer there yawned every so often and kept taking short walks to keep himself awake. If there *was* disease about, Venus knew she risked getting seriously ill. But if her theory was right, she would be safe from infection.

Venus watched him from the safety of the trees on the other side of the road. She was thirty metres away and well hidden. The next nearest officer was round a corner. He'd never see her.

Ten minutes later, when the nearest officer started coughing, she saw her chance. He reached into his trouser pocket and pulled out a handkerchief which he clumsily dropped on to the damp grass.

As he knelt down, Venus moved.

She flew across the road and climbed over the low barbed-wire fence. She took a couple of steps forward and listened. The policeman was still coughing.

She crept stealthily forward.

Picking her way through the dense mass of trees, Venus kept low. She'd heard Dennis and Alan describing the layout of the farm. She reckoned she could get to the animal barns and the lake – and be back at Riley Croft within forty minutes.

The farmhouse came into view. The kitchen light was on and she saw Alan's silhouette at the window. He was holding a phone. Venus thought about Annie and shivered.

She tiptoed over towards a row of barns. Crouching low so as not to be seen, she pulled the bag off her shoulder and got the equipment out.

It didn't take long.

She followed the path to her left, which ran beyond the farmhouse to a line of trees. A minute later, she saw the water of the lake shimmering in the moonlight. She reached for the equipment again.

When she was done, she quickly checked and checked her findings again. It was worse than she'd thought. She felt a thread of panic inside her. Kate was right. Things were getting far too dangerous. She needed to tell Dennis. Now. Carefully she dried the equipment on the sleeve of her coat.

She was kneeling down and putting the equipment back in her bag when she suddenly felt something cool and metallic pressing sharply against her cheek. She glanced sideways. It was the barrel of a shotgun.

The gun was held by a large, shaven-headed man with a misshapen nose. He wore a tweed cap and had a slightly manic look in his green eyes. A finger was on his lips.

'Make a sound and say goodbye to your head,' he whispered. He raised a finger indicating for Venus to stand up. She did so slowly, the gun barrel still pushing against her cheek.

She considered screaming. The farmhouse wasn't that far away and they'd be bound to hear her. But what if he was trigger happy or even fired in shock?

The man opened his mouth and revealed several

blackened teeth. 'You must be one of Joe Thorn's kids?' he said gruffly. 'And you're on my patch.'

Venus slowly looked down. On the ground, next to his feet, was a large wire net with some dead chickens inside. He looked like he was some sort of poacher – Venus had once seen a documentary about them at school.

She shook her head carefully, the gun barrel moving with her head. The name Joe Thorn sounded familiar, but she couldn't recall how she knew it.

'I don't know anyone called Joe Thorn,' she replied shakily, her facial muscles taut with fear. 'And anyway, you must have seen the police round the farm. Every bird round here has probably got that disease.'

Venus winced as the gun barrel bit further into her cheek, her mind going over any possible methods of escape.

'Doesn't bother me. I'll sell those birds miles from – here no one will have a clue. Anyway, your friend Joe would do exactly the same thing. But you'd know all about that, wouldn't you?'

'Joe Thorn's got nothing to do with me,' Venus replied with terror. 'If you could just move the gun away from my face, I'll be out of here and let you get on with your work.'

He eased the barrel a fraction away from Venus's

cheek. 'I don't like the thought of you telling any of those policemen about me.'

'I won't tell anyone. I promise,' Venus whispered. 'People on the farm have got more important things to worry about – like the farmer's daughter, Annie. She might already be dead.'

A look of anxiety momentarily passed over the man's face, but the cold-hearted expression soon returned.

'I can't let you go,' he said with menace, cocking the gun. The metallic click made Venus start.

He raised the butt of the rifle.

Venus acted instantly. She sprang backwards, her body arching in a backflip while simultaneously stretching out her right leg and kicking the gun out of his hands. The weapon whistled through the air, landing on the ground behind him.

Then he lunged at her.

She sidestepped his outstretched body, grabbed her bag off the ground and ran. She looked back for a second and saw him scooping the gun off the floor. Then he tore after her. Venus sped through the undergrowth.

'Come back here!' hissed the man furiously, his footsteps crunching speedily after her.

The branches ripped into Venus's face as she ran.

She was heading in the opposite direction to the way she came. She was totally disorientated. She had to get out of the farm, but now she didn't have just the police to worry about – she had a crazed gun-toting poacher to deal with.

As she fled, she suddenly heard a crack from behind. A rush of air hurtled past her ear and a thwacking sound splintered on one of the trees ahead.

It was a bullet. He'd fired at her! He was completely mad.

Venus accelerated rapidly. The branches were coming thicker and faster, restricting her movement. She could hear the poacher panting behind her, his footsteps thundering forwards. And now she could hear voices, coming from somewhere to her right.

Another bullet flashed past her, missing her right ear by a couple of centimetres before disappearing into a bush.

A booming voice suddenly called out: 'STOP NOW! THIS IS THE POLICE.'

The poacher was gaining on her.

'THIS SITE IS COMPLETELY SURROUNDED BY POLICE OFFICERS,' called the voice. 'PUT DOWN YOUR WEAPON!'

The thought of stopping and alerting the police to

her presence tempted Venus for a second but she knew that would make her a sitting target for the poacher.

'WE ARE ARMED OFFICERS! PUT DOWN YOUR WEAPON!'

Another bullet careered just above her shoulder. Venus crashed forward, frantically searching for any sign of a fence. She could hear the poacher growling and swearing over her shoulder. She couldn't chance him taking another shot at her.

'THIS IS THE POLICE! YOU HAVE NOWHERE TO GO!' the voice called again, much nearer this time. A pinpoint of light flashed through the undergrowth.

'Over there!' shouted another voice. 'He's got some sort of rifle.'

The poacher's footsteps were catching up with her and the police was closing in on both of them.

'PUT DOWN THE WEAPON!'

Venus could hear the breathing of the poacher behind her. He couldn't be more than ten metres away.

Beams of light criss-crossed through the dense trees on the farm side of the road. And then she suddenly saw a stretch of wire fencing dotted with red circles, electrified – to keep cattle in.

Venus hurtled forward. The fence was now only five metres away. She could hear the low hum of its electrical voltage. How bad would it be if she gave her pursuer and the police the slip, only to be fried trying to hurdle a cattle fence? She spied an overhanging branch.

Venus flew forward and reached out for the branch. *Thank God I've watched Kelly Tanner's jump over the prison perimeter wire in* Forest Breakout, *ten thousand times.*

Venus's hands momentarily gripped the rough bark and she swung forward, clearing the fence and landing with a thud on the grass beyond it.

Ahead of her was a narrow mossy path. She sped across it and disappeared into the trees at the top of a grass bank.

'PUT YOUR WEAPON DOWN!'

Venus pushed on. She didn't have time to wait and see what happened to the gun-toting psycho poacher.

🏃 Chapter 25

22.23

'Dad?'

'Gail, everything OK?'

'Venus's mobile keeps saying "number un-obtainable".'

'We sometimes have bad reception out here,' Dennis replied.

'Well, there was something else I wanted to ask you.'

'Fire away.'

'Has Venus had some sort of falling out with a boy called Franco?'

Dennis remembered the cut on Venus's cheek at the end of the sword-fighting session. There was no point in mentioning this to Gail – she'd only worry unnecessarily. It was a good thing, too, news of what was happening at Riley Croft was being kept quiet.

'Not that I know of, love,' he answered, 'but you know kids – they're all hormones and mood swings. I don't think it would have been anything serious.'

'You sure?'

'Yep,' he answered uncertainly.

'OK, Dad.'

'Night, kid.'

'Don't call me "kid".'

23.00

Venus took in her bearings. She had made it to the other side of the farm. Its perimeter fence stretched behind her. She just hoped that the police had got to the poacher. If they hadn't, he could be anywhere out here.

She looked around nervously for any sign of him, but the only shapes she saw were the huge trees.

Once again, she felt frightened and alone. She wondered about the wisdom of not sharing her concerns. Why hadn't she just told Dennis everything? Why not Jed? The trouble was, she was used to keeping secrets – telling lies to her mum about where she was and what she was doing. Thinking of Mum in London made Venus suddenly feel even worse. If only she hadn't got herself into this mess. This wasn't some big budget movie where she could now go and take a break in her trailer.

This was real.

Which way should she go?

Left or right or straight ahead?

It was impossible to tell. She'd have to make a wild guess.

Opting for right, she ran through the thicket of trees until she reached a narrow road. Turning left on to it, she jogged – sticking to the bank and swivelling her head every few seconds to check for any signs of the poacher.

As her feet connected with the tarmac, Venus felt the bag over her shoulder and shuddered at the thought of what she'd found on the farm. If she didn't get word to people pretty soon . . .

As she reached the brow of a hill, something appeared in front of her like an oasis in the middle of a scorching desert. A phone box. It was one of those old-fashioned sorts; red with a dome-shaped top. It stood on a mound of grass, seemingly in the middle of nowhere. There must be a village nearby, Venus reckoned as she sprinted down the hill. But there was no sign of one. She quickly thought of all the vandalised phone boxes back home.

Please let it be working.

She pulled open the heavy door and dropped her bag on to the floor. Snatching the receiver she breathed a huge sigh of relief. The dialling tone sounded in her ear.

She frantically started punching in the numbers of Dennis's mobile. She was about to press the two last digits when she heard the revving of a motorbike. It had a familiar and reassuring tone.

It was Dennis's bike. He must have discovered she was gone again without his permission. He'd definitely freak out but, when she revealed what she knew, surely he'd understand the importance of her mission and go easy on her?

The revving sounded again and relief swam through her body. She replaced the receiver and reached down to pick her bag off the floor. As her fingers gripped the top of her bag, the bike revved once more, far louder than before. She grabbed her bag and saw that the bike was picking up speed and advancing.

It was heading straight *towards* the telephone box.

What was Dennis up to? Surely now was no time for stunt tricks?

She reached for the door. The bike thundered forward. She pushed the door further open.

The bike was now hurtling towards her incredibly fast, its beam blinding.

The door was more than halfway open when the bike caught it with a glancing blow, flinging Venus backwards. She hit her shoulder against the receiver unit and dropped to the floor.

The bike pulled back and sped away.

Shock coursed through Venus's body as the terrible truth struck her. The rider wasn't Dennis. It must be the poacher.

He'd evaded the police and mounted Dennis's motorbike or one strikingly similar in size and sound. Maybe he'd been to Riley Croft earlier and stolen Dennis's machine? But why wasn't he using his gun? Had he run out of bullets?

Before Venus could stand up properly the bike had already turned round and was heading back towards the phone box.

She stood up and pushed at the door. It had buckled

slightly on impact with the bike and jammed. She barged her shoulder against it as hard as she could, but it didn't give. It was locking her into a prison of certain death. She shoved it again with her shoulder, but it wouldn't budge.

She whacked her shoulder against the door, in desperation.

The headlight was flashing towards her again and she ducked down to the floor. She'd be lucky to avoid this second onslaught without sustaining a serious injury. Crouching, she covered her head with her hands in terror as the bike pounded straight into the door with a vicious smack, smashing out all the windows. Pieces of glass flew around her body and into her hair.

The bent metal door caved inwards, missing her knees by a fraction of a centimetre. Tears of terror were streaming down her face. Her heart was thumping in overdrive. The bike backed off then spun round as it prepared for a third crack at its target.

This time it would get her. The door would crush her to death.

In an instant Venus was back on her feet, the menacing outline of the bike starting towards her once more. She leaned back against the receiver before unleashing a two-footed kick against the door. It moved a fraction. The bike was bearing down on her, faster and faster.

She kicked out again, and the twisted metal seemed to groan as the door moved slightly further. But it wasn't moving far enough. With a last desperate surge, Venus braced herself for a final kick.

The bike crashed forward. It was now nearly upon her.

As her feet kicked out for the third desperate time, the door flung open and Venus dived out of the box and rolled on to the grass to her left. A split-second later the bike careered inside the phone box, smashing against the receiver unit.

The wheels screeched as they spun over the floor of the phone box. The driver was slumped over the front of the bike.

To Venus's left was a narrow track with a public footpath sign at its mouth. She ran towards it as the angry roar of the bike's engine gasped and choked behind her.

🏃 Chapter 26

23.16

'How on earth did he get in there?' Detective Chief

Inspector Radcliff's voice was filled with disbelief and anger.

The road signs flew by the police car in the darkness.

'We don't know,' replied the voice on the phone. 'He must have just slipped in.'

'You let a man carrying a gun *just slip in*?' Radcliff sighed. 'Well, what does the suspect have to say for himself?'

There was silence at the other end of the line.

'Don't tell me he got away?'

'I'm afraid so.'

'There's eight of you! Find him and make sure that the site is properly secured. Do I make myself clear?'

'Absolutely.'

DCI Radcliff clicked her phone off and pressed down hard on the car's accelerator.

23.44

Venus's feet were soaking. Her face was hot with sweat and dirt. She untangled pieces of glass from her matted hair as she ran.

Starting on the public footpath, Venus had taken as many turns as possible, crossing a huge cornfield, leaping over a stream and zigzagging down a dusty dirt track. She'd passed several old shacks and outbuildings, but there had been no sign of any human habitation.

Just when she felt tiredness completely overwhelm her, Venus spotted a barn. She was too exhausted to move on, so she walked up to it. The barn stood behind a low wooden fence, isolated and still in the black night. She wearily jumped the fence and walked a hundred metres beyond it to check for a farmhouse or cottage, but there was nothing. She jogged back to the barn.

The door gave easily.

As her eyes adjusted to the dimness, she could make out thousands of logs stacked in great piles and pinned in by other logs. They were so neatly arranged that they didn't look real – they could have been giant toy bricks awaiting the hands of a toddler.

She shut the door behind her and walked in. At the far side was a wooden ladder, propped up against a wooden ledge jutting out over the log store. She placed her foot on the first rung and scaled the ladder, easing herself on to the hay matting at the top. Gripping the ladder with both hands, she pulled it up and slid it alongside her. Then she crawled right to the edge of the hay and rolled over. As she lay back looking up at the wooden roofing slats of the barn, images from the night flashed through her brain.

Don't fall asleep, Venus commanded herself. *Don't fall asleep.*

But however wired her mind was, the sweeping pull of exhaustion kicked into her body and it wasn't long before her eyelids lowered and she tumbled into sleep.

DAY TEN

🏃 Chapter 27

00.30

When Venus woke her neck ached. She shivered with cold. Her teeth chattered. Her eyes were about to shut again, when she was alerted by the sound of a swift movement coming from somewhere beneath her. Not daring to risk detection by crawling and looking over the edge, she waited. There was silence for a few seconds and then another noise.

Footsteps.

Memories of the poacher came flooding back to her and she shifted uneasily. Had he somehow managed to follow her here?

Get a grip. It's more likely to be a farmer.

There was quiet again for at least a minute, and Venus was beginning to feel the first shoots of relief when the footsteps started up again. Only this time they were nearer, and crossing the barn in her direction.

She edged backwards, pressing against the wall. The footsteps stopped again. They were now almost directly beneath. Then she heard of an object being dragged across the floor. What was it? A log? A piece of machinery? She didn't have to wait long because a few seconds later the object came into view.

It was another ladder.

🏃 Chapter 28

00.32

The silver-eyed woman dragged the package across the field. She approached the large building in front of her and slid open the door. The space inside was gloomy and silent. She walked in, sticking to the right wall.

About fifty metres in, a large shape loomed over her. She pulled a small torch from her pocket and shone it into the darkness. The beam was surprisingly strong and illuminated a great white circle. She walked a few paces forward and then placed the package on the ground. It was wrapped in a thick cardboard tube that came off easily. Her torch pinpointed the exact spot she needed.

After months of waiting she was now only minutes away.

The ladder's top three rungs were visible. Venus stared in horror as she heard feet beginning to ascend. She looked desperately around her, but there was nowhere to hide. She could spring forward and push the ladder over, but what if it was an innocent farmer, simply carrying out some midnight chore?

The feet climbed further and then the top of someone's head came into view.

But it wasn't the poacher or a farmer.

'Fancy meeting you here,' said a familiar voice.

Venus's pupils dilated with shock. 'F. . . r . . . r . . . anco,' she spluttered.

He spoke calmly. 'Come down, Venus.'

'What are you doing here?' she asked nervously.

'I followed you,' he replied softly.

Venus felt a chill encasing every bone in her body. It felt weird to hear Franco speaking to her without a scowl on his face. 'Why?'

'I thought you might be in some sort of trouble.'

He's lying. Think about all of the things you've seen. He's up to his neck in it.

'Yeah?' Venus asked suspiciously.

'Look Venus, I'm telling the truth. We're never going to be best friends, but we are on the same camp. I wouldn't want anything bad to happen to you.'

Venus stared into his eyes. Could she possibly have got it all wrong about Franco? Had her imagination been working overtime? Was there a perfectly simple explanation for everything? Her weary body certainly yearned for one. The sooner this ordeal was over, the better.

'I lost you when you were on Docker's farm,' Franco continued, gripping the rungs of the ladder. 'But when I heard those gunshots, I panicked. I saw you vaulting over that electric fence so I picked up your trail again.'

Venus's mind ached. *Could it be true? What about their sword fight, the trip on the platform, his constant hostility? They were enemies – weren't they?*

'What happened after that?' she asked.

'I was quite a long way behind you, but when I got to that top of the hill I saw that madman on the motorbike attacking you.'

'You saw that?' Venus recalled the terror of the phone box.

'It was shocking.' Franco nodded earnestly. 'It was like watching a horror movie. I ran down the hill, but by the time I got there, the front of the bike was smashed inside the phone box and you were running off down a footpath.'

'Was anyone on the bike?' Venus asked.

Franco shook his head. 'Not that I saw.'

In the dim light of the barn, his face looked so sincere. A part of her screamed out not to trust anything he said, but another part so wanted to believe him.

Venus was torn. She longed to be back with Dennis, but surely being taken in by Franco was a seriously dangerous strategy?

'We can be back at Riley Croft in an hour,' said Franco soothingly.

Venus thought about hot showers, fresh clothes and the warmth of the dorm at Riley Croft. It was very tempting.

Should she? Shouldn't she?

Franco looked up at her imploringly.

She stared at him silently for a few moments. 'OK,' she agreed, slowly nodding her head, but thinking she'd have to be a hundred per cent on her guard.

Franco climbed down. Venus swung her legs out over the ladder and followed him. As her feet reached the barn floor, she turned round. Franco was standing a few feet away, his face formed into a half-smile. Venus caught his gaze but, as she did so, his expression suddenly transformed into a totally different type of smile.

An evil one.

Venus swore at herself. She looked back at the

ladder, but Franco quickly pushed it over. It thudded to the ground.

If only I'd stayed up in the hayloft. Then I'd have had the advantage of height. I could have kicked him off the ladder before he could get anywhere near me.

Instead, she now stood only a few feet away from him. And although she knew she was a match for him physically, her body wasn't in its greatest state for a fight. Her bones felt like they'd been run over by an express train.

'Thought you were being some sort of detective, didn't you?' Franco snarled, taking a step forward.

Venus stared as he reached in to his pocket and produced Dennis's motorbike keys.

'It was you?' she gasped.

'Dennis really shouldn't leave his keys lying around in the canteen.'

'You tried to kill me back there,' Venus whispered, fear strangling her throat.

'Whatever you say.' His smile was sour and vengeful.

Venus quickly checked out the layout of the barn. The door was the only one exit and there were no windows – just thousands of neatly stacked logs. Unless she could talk her way out of this, things weren't looking too good.

'Listen,' began Venus. 'I don't know what you're mixed up in but it's not too late to pull out. I can help you.'

Franco snorted. 'The only one who needs help round here is you!'

Venus took a step back.

'You've been very lucky, Venus,' Franco said with a sneer, taking another step towards her. 'But also stupid. You should have minded your own business.'

Venus felt a giant knot twisting and turning in her stomach. She racked her brains for a strategy.

'We can find a way out of this, Franco,' she said calmly.

'No, we can't,' he snapped. 'Your interference could spoil everything.' He edged even closer, his eyes flashing with menace.

'What do you mean?' Venus asked.

'You know exactly what I mean,' he said.

'Let's go back to the site and sort this out,' Venus said quickly, retreating further.

Franco laughed cruelly. 'You don't get it, do you?' His eyes were red with fury. 'I was too slipshod with the bike. I'm not going to make that mistake again.'

'NO, FRANCO!' Venus shouted as she stumbled backwards against one of the giant wooden pillars holding up the barn.

Franco stepped forward and reached out to grab Venus by the throat.

At that instant, Venus grabbed the wooden pillar with both hands; she swivelled around it and kicked a vertical log to her left.

It was pinning back a massive pile of other logs.

As her feet made impact, the 'locking in' log lifted up and slipped its catch. Immediately a riot of noise erupted and logs started cascading down.

The sound was deafening. Venus flung herself out of the way on to the ground and escaped the onslaught by a millimetre.

But Franco wasn't so lucky.

He cried out for a second but was immediately silenced as log after log piled down on him, violently knocking him to the ground and crashing on top of him.

Venus lay on the ground, unable to move or think. The uproar continued for at least a minute and when it had stopped, a thick film of sawdust covered the entire barn. She coughed and brushed the dust from her face.

When the last log had finally rolled across some others and settled, the barn became eerily quiet. Venus gaped at the devastation. Wood was strewn all over the floor. Where Franco had been standing was a mound of logs. She rose slowly and it was then that she saw it.

It looked like some grotesque sculpture by a headline-grabbing punk artist.

A still, lifeless hand was sticking up through a gap in the log mountain.

It was drained of all colour.

Venus put her hand over her mouth and stared in horror as the terrible truth struck her.

Franco was dead.

🏃 Chapter 29

00.44

Venus ran.

The trees to her left towered above, a blur of dark greens and browns. The black sky seemed to lurch menacingly down towards her, as if it would swallow her whole body if she stopped. Tears streamed down her cheeks as her mind kept replaying the image of the lifeless hand jutting up through the logs.

Her heart pounded furiously.

I killed Franco.

She pictured a dimly lit courtroom, a lawyer twisting her words and unravelling her guilt. She saw herself locked in a dank, filthy, cold cell – isolated and afraid.

She jumped over a fence, just missing a tree to her

right. Her judgement was foggy; her brain let loose from its moorings.

She dropped to the ground, rested her back against a giant, gnarled oak tree and closed her eyes. Her thoughts crashed around inside her head, fighting each other to be heard.

If I hadn't done something he would have killed me first. But it was my kick that crushed him to death. I didn't set out to hurt him – it just happened. I'm going to spend the rest of my life behind bars.

'Stop!' she shouted out loud, silencing her mind for a second.

She reached into her jacket pocket and fumbled for a tissue, but her hand came into contact with something else.

She pulled it out. The map from the common room.

Get it together, Venus. Franco is dead. There's nothing you can do about it. Use the map and get back to Riley Croft.

She wiped the sweat off her forehead and pushed her hair tighter into her hairband. The moonlight made it possible to see the map, which she unfolded and spread on the ground in front of her. Her mind was still spinning, but she forced herself to concentrate. Desperately seeking a landmark, she rotated the map several times until she spotted the cut of trees on the far side of the field. OK. She'd pinpointed where she was.

Checking the scale, she reckoned she was a couple of miles away from Riley Croft.

She was about to close the map, when something suddenly sprang into her head. She looked at the numbers surrounding the map and recalled the four digits on Franco's text message. 3205.

She looked down at the map again. 3205.

The numbers were staring her in the face. They were map coordinates.

Quickly she ran her finger over the map and located the point at which the coordinates converged – the middle of a large expanse of green labelled AIRFIELD (DISUSED). It was about a mile away.

She sat still for a moment – thinking whether or not she should turn back and try to find Dennis. But she was far too deeply in this. She had to go on – at least a bit further.

Ten minutes later she was standing in front of a high wooden fence, staring out over a deep and wide parcel of land. She climbed over the fence and walked to the start of a long concrete path, covered in moss and thistles. *This must be the old runway.* It looked like it hadn't seen any action for years.

To her right, a few hundred yards away, were two giant aircraft hangars.

She stopped in front of the first hangar. It was covered with graffiti. Its huge sliding doors were open a fraction – enough for a person to get through. For a second Venus thought she heard a sound coming from inside. She shook her head. It was just the moaning of the wind. She stepped inside and let her eyes adjust to the light. The hangar was completely empty.

She decided to try the second hangar. If there was nothing there, she'd go straight back to Riley Croft. She was about to turn round when from behind her a powerful arm gripped her tightly round the throat. She tried to yell out, but no sound came out. She lashed out with her arms, but the grip just got tighter. As she stopped struggling she saw the markings on the arm that held her. An intricate seafaring tattoo.

And on her assailant's finger was the snake ring. Before Venus could try any other means of escape, there was a sudden blow to her head.

The next thing she saw was blackness.

🏃 Chapter 30

01.15

Venus opened her eyes for a moment. Her head throbbed and her mouth crackled with thirst. It took her a few seconds to remember the tattooed arm squeezing the breath out of her. She tried to reach up to soothe her aching throat, but discovered her arms were firmly tied behind her back. Her feet were bound too. She was in some sort of wooden cabin. There were a few old packing crates stacked up against the wall opposite her. At the far side of the room was the top of a staircase that headed downwards and out of sight. The only window in the room was to the left of the staircase. She looked up, preparing to face the naval man from the pub.

There was the tattoo and the snake ring. But Venus now realised they hadn't been on the arm and finger of a man. They belonged to a woman. She was dressed in combat gear and army boots. Her hair was short and blond. But what struck Venus most were the woman's eyes. They were silver. They looked unreal, as if they'd been coloured in by a street artist. She was sitting on an upturned crate, eyeing Venus studiously.

'How the hell did you find out about this place?' the woman asked. Her voice was cold and harsh.

'Can I have a drink of water?' croaked Venus.

'No,' snapped the woman, 'not before you tell me why you came here.'

'I got lucky.'

'Got lucky? I think not.' The woman sneered. 'I'd

say you've got yourself involved in an extremely dangerous game.'

'I'm not playing a game,' Venus replied, her throat scratching with each syllable she uttered. 'I really need a drink.'

'Tell me how you got here.'

'I told you already – it was luck. But there's no point keeping me here. The police will be here any minute. I've already called them.'

'*Liar!*' screamed the woman, slamming the heels of her boots against the crate. 'I saw to it that your mobile disappeared. No mobile. No call to the police.'

Venus tried not to show the fear she felt in the pit of her stomach. 'I'm not lying,' she insisted, 'and I don't think the police will look too kindly on someone who ties up fourteen-year-olds.'

'*Be quiet,*' snarled the woman. 'Where's Franco?'

'I don't know.' Venus tried to keep an even rhythm in her voice, afraid that the slightest quiver would somehow give her guilt away.

'When was the last time you saw him?'

'Just after supper,' Venus lied, 'and I don't know why you keep on calling him that. Franco Dane wasn't his real name.'

The woman's eyes bored into Venus like sharpened spikes. 'What did you just say?' she hissed. She stood up and walked over to Venus, crouching down directly in front of her. Her hot breath smelled of mints and stale cigarettes. 'You said *wasn't*, what do you mean *wasn't*?'

The woman's expression was suspicious and accusing. Venus instantly wished she'd kept her mouth shut. Maybe that would have given her a better chance to escape.

'Wasn't, isn't – it makes no difference,' Venus replied quickly. 'But what was he doing at stunt camp? And how's he mixed up with all of this?'

A slow, cruel smile played across the woman's lips. 'Do you really think I could let a fifteen-year-old boy stay at a hotel or bed and breakfast by himself? He'd stick out a mile. When I found out about stunt camp, I discovered a great opportunity. He's agile and fast. Why not stick him in there with some other teenagers so he'd blend in.'

The woman paused for a few seconds. 'At least that's the way I planned it.'

'What you're doing is evil,' Venus hissed.

'Spare me the morality tale,' shouted the woman, leaning forward and grabbing Venus's chin in her hand. 'Some pathetic people play by the rules and end up with nothing. I go after what I want. And if some-one's in the way, then . . .'

'So where did you find Franco?' asked Venus, playing for time. 'Did you cradlesnatch him from some young offenders institution?'

The woman slapped Venus hard across the face. Her cut cheek stung with pain.

The woman stared at Venus with hate-filled eyes and slowly stood up. 'If you really must know, he's my son,' she said quietly.

Venus swallowed hard. This psycho woman didn't look like the kind of person who'd deal gently with her child's killer.

'What are you going to do with me?' Venus asked quietly.

The woman glared at her. 'You'll pay for your interference.' She stood and looked like she was about to make an exit.

'Just untie me,' begged Venus. 'When the police find out about all this, they'll take into account the fact that you let me go.'

The woman did up her jacket and stared at Venus. 'Don't you get it? There will be no police. My tracks will be so well covered that they won't have the tiniest idea about my role in this affair.'

With this, the silver-eyed woman pulled out a lighter from her jacket pocket. Venus felt a ripple of terror. She looked around the room. Everything was made of wood. It was an arsonist's dream. The woman clicked the lighter and a yellowy-orange flame sprang up.

Venus felt the panic rise in her chest. 'You can't do this,' she urged in a strangled voice. 'You'll never get away with it.'

'I will,' the woman said, smiling.

Venus struggled furiously to loosen the ropes on her hands. But the knots were far too tight. The whole place would go up in minutes. She'd be burned to a crisp. The lighter illuminated the woman's face and the flame's reflection danced in her silver eyes.

'No!' yelled Venus.

The woman knelt down and let the lighter flame come into contact with the floor. It took a few seconds, but a wooden plank lit up and the first wisps of smoke drifted upwards.

'Please!' yelled Venus in terror. The smoke would kill her before the flames consumed her. She frantically pulled at the ropes again. They didn't shift at all.

'Goodbye,' whispered the woman, walking towards the top of the staircase. With that, she hurried down and out of view. Venus heard her footsteps clanking down the stairs, followed by the sound of a door slamming shut.

Venus stared round the room. The flame on the first

lit floorboard was rising steadily and the fire was spreading onto the adjacent floorboards with a menacing crackle.

The smoke was already getting into Venus's mouth and lungs. She coughed. She wouldn't be able to last more than a few minutes in here. It was over.

Chapter 31

01.24

Jed woke up. He slipped out of bed and put on his jacket and shoes to go to the toilet. He walked across the dorm and was about to open the door, when he noticed how flat the shape of Franco's body looked on his bed.

He moved over and pulled the blankets back. Beneath them were a rucksack and a pair of shoes laid out carefully to resemble the shape of a human body.

Jed suddenly remembered Venus's words from earlier. *'I know all about you, Franco Dane.'* And then he recalled seeing Venus kick the foil out of Franco's grasp. Jed felt fear twist in his stomach. He dropped the blankets and hurried out of the dorm. He ran down the path to the girls' dorm and opened the door, creeping over to Venus's bed.

She hadn't even tried to make it look like someone was asleep there. Her bunk was empty too.

Jed tried not to panic, but he sensed that something seriously bad was going on. He belted across to Dennis's cabin and knocked on the door. There was no reply. He knocked harder. Footsteps sounded inside. The door opened and a bleary-eyed Dennis appeared.

'What's going on?' he asked.

'There's something you need to know,' Jed replied urgently.

🏃 Chapter 32

01.25

Venus was coughing and spluttering, her breathing strained and painful. The fire was moving steadily in her direction.

Frantically, she looked around the room. She struggled with the ropes around her hands and feet. As the panic rose in her she suddenly spotted something. It was a long, thin piece of wood sitting on top of one of the packing crates. The fire hadn't reached that wall yet.

It wasn't much, but it was her only hope.

She started shuffling across the floor on her knees.

It was agonisingly slow and painful, but she made it over. Leaning forward slowly, she clamped her teeth around the thin piece of wood. She eased down onto her front and moved across the floor *towards* the fire. The heat increased with every move. Her face was scorching. When she was only centimetres away from the flames she leaned her head forward, holding out the thin piece of wood with her mouth.

It took about a minute, but the piece of wood caught. Venus backed away before putting her face to the ground and wedging the stick between two floor-boards with the flame pointing up. She turned and held her hands out behind her back towards the flame. The heat was intense and it seemed to take for ever to burn through the rope. Meanwhile, the room was becoming smothered in flames and smoke.

With her hands being scalded by the flames, suddenly the rope came loose. She'd done it! But she had to untie her feet. She could hardly move her hands – the rope had been so tight on them – but she forced them downwards and began desperately pulling at the ropes around her feet. Again and again she pulled, but the smoke curled further into her body while flames threatened to devour her.

But on her seventh attempt, the leg ropes loosened a fraction and with several extra tugs, they came free.

Venus screamed in terror as the searing heat clung to her body. Her back was on fire.

It was go now – or die.

She charged wildly forward, her limbs just about obeying her. She leaped through the crazed flames.

Please let me have judged it right.

Her body shattered the glass panes as she careered through the window frame at the far side of the room and fell out on to the grass below. A human torch, she rolled over on to her back, screeching in terror and pain.

As she gasped in lungfuls of the cool fresh air, Dennis's voice hurdled through her brain. He always said it when working with fire.

Starve the flame.

She thrashed around on the grass frantically beating at the flames on her back.

The fire fought back viciously, the heat raging across her sweatshirt.

Starve the flame.

Adrenalin was coursing through Venus and she found hidden resources of strength and determination. Repeatedly, she rolled on the grass. Gradually she gained the upper hand and the flames began to recede. With three more rolls she managed to put out the last traces of fire.

She lay on the ground, breathing hard and feeling

the scorching heat still on her back. Looking up she saw the towering wooden watchtower above her, completely shrouded by flames and smoke. Any longer in there and she'd have been ash.

She sat up and pulled off her sweatshirt. It was completely covered in holes and burnt patches. She moved her body slightly and realised that by some miracle, she hadn't suffered any serious burns on her back and that her T-shirt was still intact.

Her throat felt as though it had been sand-papered. She was disorientated, bewildered and shaken.

But none of this stopped her hearing the low rumbling sound in the distance.

🏃 Chapter 33

01.29

Jed paced about the site office nervously. When would Dennis be back? What had happened to Venus and Franco?

The moment he'd told Dennis they were missing, Dennis had sprung into action. He'd urged Jed to say nothing to the others. As they ran to the site office, Dennis had asked, 'Have you got any idea where either of them might have gone?'

Jed had shaken his head.

As they'd reached the office, Dennis had stopped dead in his tracks. 'My motorbike's gone,' he'd said in a hushed whisper.

'No way,' Jed replied.

But Dennis was already unlocking the office's padlock and flinging the door open. 'Stay in here in case they show up,' he commanded.

And with that, Dennis had gone.

🏃 Chapter 34

01.30

The low rumbling sound was the revving of an engine. A few seconds later, a small plane emerged from the second aircraft hangar. Venus recognised it immediately. It was a Cessna – a four-seat twin-engine plane. She'd spent two days watching a Cessna being stormed by 'terrorists', when Dennis was stunt coordinator on *Flying Death*, a film about corruption in the US Air Force.

But it wasn't the Cessna itself that grabbed her attention. It was the item on its underside – a large canister with a dark green cross on its top half, exactly like the sign on the thin tube she'd seen Franco holding in the pub. But this time Venus could see the other symbol.

It was the skull and crossbones.

She stared in horror as the plane began to taxi up the old runway, bumping along over the moss and thistles. Venus needed to get to the plane before it was going too fast.

It took the plane a minute to reach the end of the runway before turning round. In a few moments it would start back down the runway, accelerating rapidly for take-off. Venus knew the silver-eyed woman would be speaking now to local air traffic control, making the final checks before take-off.

Venus ran forward, the wind whipping furiously at her ears. Each step was agony, her smoke-filled chest cutting into her breathing, her body aching. The plane was accelerating fast. In seconds she'd miss it.

As Venus got nearer the plane, she saw that the silver-eyed woman was wearing earphones and an old-fashioned pilot's helmet. She could also see the canister more clearly now. It had a nozzle at its tip.

By the time Venus was within touching distance of the plane, the revving of the engines suddenly became deafening. The plane prepared for take-off. Venus dived forward, grabbing the top of the wing with her hands while planting her feet on the metal strut just above one of the plane's wheels.

At that second, the plane began to hurtle down the runway. Venus's left hand lost its grip on the top side of the wing and for a moment it felt like she was going to fall. But she grasped the wing again and began to pull herself upwards as the plane thundered forward. As Venus strengthened her grip, the plane's nose rose into the air and the Cessna left the runway.

The wind blew ferociously in Venus's face as she carefully pulled herself up onto the wing. Crouching down to keep her centre of gravity low, she started inching along the wing towards the cockpit.

When she was halfway along the wing, the silver-eyed woman suddenly turned around and spotted her with a look of stunned disbelief. Venus steadied herself and edged further forward.

The woman grabbed the plane's controls and pulled furiously. Venus knew at once what the woman was attempting. She was going to turn the plane over – hurling Venus to her death. Venus clenched her fists and stepped forward quickly. She needed to grab hold of something. The plane was turning sharply and Venus slid a few paces. Another move like that and she'd be history. Her body was shaking, her legs wobbled. The woman pulled harder at the controls.

Venus leaped forward and grabbed the silver catch

on the cockpit door. She yanked at it and the door flung open. Instinctively, the woman lashed out, her blow catching Venus on the forehead. Venus reeled back, almost losing her footing on the wing's smooth surface. But she clung onto the cockpit door with her right hand. The woman's arm came smashing down and reels of pain shot up Venus's hand and arm.

But her grip remained.

Instantly the woman brought her fist down for another attack, but Venus was too quick this time. In a split second, she pulled her right hand out of the way, while simultaneously grasping the cockpit door with her left hand. The woman's blow landed on the edge of the cockpit door. Above the great bellowing noise of the wind and the engines, Venus heard her howl in pain.

Without waiting for the next attack, Venus jutted her head inside the cockpit. She held the door with her left hand and reached inside the cockpit with her right hand.

Her fingertips were inches away from the controls when the woman gripped Venus round the neck with one hand and squeezed. Venus felt her lifeline of oxygen being cut off.

Venus's next move was borrowed from the infant playground. But it was always effective. She sank her teeth into the silver-eyed woman's hands.

The woman screamed in agony and let go of the plane's controls. The plane lurched, twisted and began to lose height.

The woman held Venus off for a second and reached out for a red button marked, *release*.

The plane hurtled downwards.

Venus recalled the canister on the underside of the Cessna. Releasing it would be the woman's grand finale.

Venus quickly let go of the cockpit door and slid down the wing. But she misjudged her speed and fell on to her back, skimming forward and to her left. She put her hands down on either side of her body and pressed hard on the wing. The friction burned her palms, but her body continued to slide forward.

She was going to fall.

But as her body shot out over the side edge of the wing, she desperately grabbed out and got hold of something round and smooth with her right arm. She looked up.

It was the canister – the deadly canister.

The plane was now roaring downward incredibly fast. Venus looked at its distance from the ground.

One hundred and fifty metres.

Venus heard a hiss. She saw with terror, the top of the canister's nozzle, slowly rotating open. The woman was unleashing her evil weapon. The second the canister opened fully, the poisonous spray would be released.

The canister's first target would be Venus's face.

She wouldn't stand a chance.

One hundred metres.

It was then that Venus spotted a blue button just above the canister. She looked down. The plane was on a terrifying collision course with the ground.

Fifty metres.

The nozzle continued to turn. Venus curled her right arm tightly round the canister.

Twenty-five metres.

The Cessna was now screaming towards the ground.

Fifteen metres.

Venus punched the blue button as hard as she could. There was a clicking sound as the canister dropped free from its slot.

She uttered a silent prayer and leaped clear of the plane.

🏃 Chapter 35

01.42

'Have you got him?' DCI Radcliff shouted into the mobile.

The car was doing well over ninety miles per hour. Radcliff had the phone in one hand and the steering wheel in the other.

'Not yet,' replied the nervous voice on the other end.

'That's not good enough. *Get him!*'

'We'll do our best,' replied the voice, weakly.

'Make sure you do!' snapped Radcliff before furiously throwing her mobile down on to the passenger seat.

🏃 Chapter 36

01.43

Venus was free-falling. With a deadly weapon tucked under her arm. But she knew where she was heading. She'd seen it as the plane swooped down.

Venus landed with a great thump on an enormous bale of hay and instinctively rolled over to cushion her fall. The plane's engines groaned as the woman tried to straighten it to begin a frantic ascent. As Venus came to a stop, the canister rolled out of her grasp. She shielded her face, waiting for the vast gush of spray to explode.

But there was silence.

She uncovered her eyes.

The canister had rolled to a stop beside another hay bale.

The nozzle remained shut.

Before Venus could move, there was suddenly a deafening explosion above her. She pulled her arms over her head. She could hear things falling to the ground. She lifted her left arm a fraction and looked up. A gigantic crimson fireball lit up the night sky, splintering streaks of red, yellow and orange in all directions.

The sky was raining metal.

The plane's fallen debris was strewn haphazardly across a large area of ground. Venus looked for a sign of the woman. But there was nothing. She might have been able to eject, but it was far more likely that she'd been burned to cinders following the explosion. Venus stood with her mouth open. A great pall of dust and smoke hung in the air as the last pieces of the plane fell.

Venus remembered the log barn and the lifeless hand.

First Franco was dead and now his mother. Venus suddenly felt overwhelmed by the enormity of the last few hours' events. She shivered as the heat of the dust cloud contrasted sharply with the cold night wind.

She took one last look at the field of destruction, then turned and ran to the edge of the field.

01.44

Jed was half asleep with his head on the office table, when he was shaken awake by a very loud noise that sounded like an explosion. He sat up wearily, wondering if anyone else had heard it or if it was just a dream. He checked his watch. It was nearly quarter to two. Dennis was still not back.

Jed suddenly felt wide awake. He walked over to a window and looked out. There was nothing but darkness to see. He started pacing round the office and with each second his anxieties got stronger. Where were Venus and Franco? What on earth was going on?

He shuddered with fear as he willed Dennis to return with some good news.

🏃 Chapter 37

02.36
'Venus!'

Dennis ran forward as his granddaughter came into view at the curve in the road. He stopped a couple of metres away from her, seeing the ash, grime and scratches on her face.

'Where the hell have you been? I thought you were dead.'

Venus stumbled forward and collapsed into his arms. As Dennis squeezed her, she felt the exhaustion and fear wash over her body.

Dennis gently released her. 'I don't know whether to be furious with you or delighted you're in one piece,' he said, his face a mesh of agonised emotions.

Venus looked over his shoulder and spied a lanky young man sporting an earnest face and a police uniform.

'PC Mark Jones,' the officer said with a nod, stepping forward a couple of paces. 'I'll take it from here, Mr Spring.'

'I had to call the police,' Dennis whispered, as the three of them walked back into the site. 'Jed woke me up and told me you and Franco weren't here. What happened? Where's Franco? Were you two together?'

Venus felt the tentacles of anxiety lashing against her chest.

'It's complicated,' she replied anxiously.

Dennis looked seriously worried.

It was only then that Venus realised her hands were shaking violently.

🏃 Chapter 38

Fifteen minutes later Venus was sitting opposite PC Jones in the site office, cradling a cup of steaming cocoa, with a blanket wrapped round her shoulders.

Dennis had asked Venus and PC Jones to wait on the road for a few minutes, while he went back into the site and sent Jed back to bed. Jed had been very reluctant at first. He was scared something had happened to Venus – he'd heard something that sounded like an explosion. But when Dennis reassured him that Venus was OK, he'd eventually accepted this and gone back to the boys' dorm.

Dennis stood in a corner of the office, watching Venus and the policeman.

'Right then,' PC Jones began in a slightly patronising tone. 'Do you know where Franco Dane is?'

Venus swallowed. 'Yes . . . well . . . kind of.'

'It's either yes or no,' the policeman replied.

'I'll take it from here, PC Jones.'

In the doorway stood a woman dressed in a black suit, her blond hair scraped back tightly on either side of her turquoise eyes. Her lips were pursed.

'DCI Carla Radcliff,' she said, entering the room. 'PC Jones, I'd like you to wait outside.'

'But, ma'am,' the officer protested, 'I've already started this interview.'

'Well, I'm unstarting it,' said Radcliff with a tough stare.

'Yes, ma'am,' Jones responded sulkily. He stomped outside, grumbling under his breath.

Radcliff shut the door. 'Hello, Dennis,' she said with a smile. She gave Dennis a hug and kissed him on the cheek.

Even though Venus was still in shock, she noticed this greeting. It looked as if Dennis and Radcliff were friends – very *close* friends. But Venus knew all of his mates and he'd never mentioned anyone called Radcliff.

'Why don't we start at the beginning?' said Radcliff, interrupting Venus's train of thought. She sat down opposite her.

Venus took a deep breath and began.

She told Radcliff about Franco's water study on his laptop, his pub meeting with the tattooed stranger, the chemical canister, the $n2O$ scrap of paper, the bio-suited woman and her initial conclusion about drug smuggling.

'Were they delivering or collecting drugs?' Radcliff asked.

'Neither.'

Radcliff looked confused.

'One night I was in the boys' dorm' Venus continued. 'There were several pairs of trousers hanging on the radiators to dry. The watermark was much higher on Franco's than on anyone else's. I couldn't work out why at first, but eventually I realised. I'd read the scribble on the paper wrongly. It wasn't an "n", it was part of an "h". It spelled H_2O – the chemical symbol for water. Then I saw the bio-hazard people. They told me that Sampson – one of Alan Docker's horses and some cows had been hit with this rare flu and that Annie had it too. But something in my brain told me that the flu thing might not be real. It might be like a sort of smokescreen.'

'What do you mean?' Radcliff asked.

'I began to ask myself, if it wasn't a disease, what the connection between Annie and the animals was. And the only thing I could think of was water. The animals drink rainwater from their troughs and Annie swims in the lake. It was just a guess but I decided to check it out. So I borrowed some water testing stuff from the classroom here and broke into the farm.'

Radcliff frowned. 'You entered the farm even though you knew it was completely restricted? Didn't it cross your mind how dangerous that was?'

'Of course,' Venus replied, 'but if I didn't get proof,

I didn't think anyone would believe me – certainly not the police. You can see the headline, can't you: *Girl on stunt camp wastes police time with imaginary tale of espionage.*'

'All right,' Radcliff conceded, 'go on.'

'I took a water reading in the trough outside Sampson's barn. The chemical balance was way off the "normal" spectrum. Then I took a reading from the lake. It was identical to the first one. I was about to set off when a poacher found me. I managed to get away from him, but he had a gun and fired it when he was chasing me.'

Dennis shook his head and muttered something inaudible under his breath.

But Radcliff had no time for reflection. 'We'll worry about the poacher later. I want to know why you took the water readings.'

Venus paused. It suddenly all seemed so far-fetched. Would Radcliff just laugh in her face?

'Franco's trousers, the H_2O thing, the canister – it just seemed to point in one direction.'

'What do you mean?' implored the DCI.

Venus hesitated. Would the DCI take her seriously?

'I . . . I . . . guessed that Franco had been standing up to his waist in the lake because he was adding something to the water.'

'Adding *what*?' asked Dennis.

'Poison,' she whispered.

Radcliff and Dennis looked at each other.

'*Poison*?' repeated Radcliff.

Venus nodded. 'The poison gives animals *and* people identical symptoms to a type of rare flu. The trough and the lake were just the beginning. The next move was to contaminate all of the water on Docker's farm.'

The room was silent for a few seconds as Radcliff and Dennis digested this shocking piece of information.

'And this plan was connected to the plane that exploded tonight?' Radcliff enquired.

'Yes,' Venus replied. 'The pilot of the plane was the one behind the whole thing. The Cessna was carrying a large canister of the poison. She was going to spray it all over Docker's farm to poison all of the water on his land. As more and more of Alan's animals and then his family began to get hit by this flu, his land would suddenly go down in value. Someone could then step in and buy it off him at a cut-down price.'

'Someone like the pilot,' Radcliff stated.

Venus nodded emphatically. 'I managed to release the canister from the plane before she opened it.'

'You were *on* the plane?' Dennis asked, stunned.

'Yes,' she said nervously, scared of Dennis's reaction.

Dennis and Radcliff both looked completely horrified and were silent for a few moments.

But Radcliff quickly tuned in again. 'OK,' she said with urgency in her voice, 'Were there any markings on the canister?'

'It said BEX590,' Venus told her. 'I memorised it.'

Radcliff was already punching a number into her mobile. '*I'm ringing the hospital where Annie is,*' she mouthed.

Radcliff was put straight through to a doctor and relayed Venus's information. When she'd finished the call, she looked at Venus. 'BEX590 is a lethal insecticide that's been banned for twenty years. Fortunately, there's an antidote. You've possibly just saved Annie's life,' she said.

Dennis held up his hand for a second. 'Let me get this straight, Venus. To bring down the value of the land, this woman, with Franco's help, was prepared to wipe out all of Alan's animals and kill people as well?'

Venus nodded.

'Have you any idea who this woman was?' asked Radcliff.

'No, but she must have something to do with buying land.'

'How is Franco connected to her?' Radcliff enquired.

'She was his mother,' Venus said quietly.

'His mother?' Radcliff raised an eyebrow. 'So where's Franco now?'

🏃 Chapter 39

03.10

The ditch was very deep. The poacher sat down and put his net of chickens on to the ground beside him. He cradled the rifle under his shoulder. They'd never find him down here.

Stupid little girl – if she hadn't turned up I'd have been home ages ago, he thought miserably.

He'd wait here for a while to be certain he was alone and then make a run for it. It was still dark – he'd be fine. He smiled greedily as he thought about the cash he'd earn from selling the dead birds. So they were infected – it wasn't his problem. He closed his eyes and dozed.

But moments later he stirred as he felt a torch beam on his eyelids. He opened his eyes slowly and looked up into the glare. It wasn't just one beam – it was a whole circle of lights. And then through the lights he saw them.

Surrounding the ditch were at least ten police officers in hard hats aiming sub-machine guns at his head.

'Throw the weapon across the ditch!' commanded a voice.

This could not be happening to him!

'I said, throw it!'

Reluctantly he flung his gun and swore loudly as a figure darted down into the ditch and grabbed it.

'Now lie face down with your hands and legs spread out.'

He slowly moved on to his knees and then lay down. Mud crumbled into his mouth. He heard feet sliding down into the ditch and a second later he felt the tough pull as handcuffs were snapped on.

This was all because of that girl.

Now he'd never get to sell those chickens.

🏃 Chapter 40

03.12

Venus had been dreading this moment. She felt her cheeks burn and her eyes sting. She turned her gaze away from Radcliff, appalled at what she was about to say.

'He's dead,' she whispered.

'What did you say?' asked Radcliff in a hushed voice.

'Dead,' Venus repeated. 'He knew I was onto them. First he tried to mow me down in a phone box on Granddad's motorbike. I escaped but then he tracked me down to a barn where I was hiding – it was some sort of log store. He was going to kill me.'

'So what did you do?' asked Dennis.

'I kicked a log that was pinning loads of others in and dived out of the way. He didn't have time to react, so he was knocked over. The logs just kept piling on top of him. When I got up, I saw his hand jutting out from beneath them. It was horrible.'

Radcliff and Dennis sat staring at Venus with their mouths wide open.

Dennis was the first to regain his composure. He reached out and touched Venus's shoulder. 'You poor girl,' he said. 'You've had a terrible experience.'

'Will I be sent to prison?' Venus asked quietly.

Radcliff looked at her for a moment without expression. 'At this stage, Venus, it *sounds* like you acted in self-defence. And it looks like Franco won't be able to give his side of the story. Did you touch anything in the barn after he died?'

'Nothing,' said Venus.

'Good. It'll make our job easier. Where is this barn?

I'll get forensics down there immediately.'

'I . . . I . . . haven't got a clue,' stuttered Venus. 'I just sort of found it.'

'Well, do you know in which direction it is?'

'I'm really sorry. It was a few miles from the old airfield, but other than that it's all a blur.'

'OK, Venus.' Radcliff nodded. 'Maybe when things have calmed down a bit, we'll see if you can remember any more. It's just that there are hundreds of barns and log stores in this area – it could take us a week to search them all.'

'Surely someone will have heard something,' said Dennis.

The DCI shook her head. 'It's the height of summer, Dennis. A lot of these places are only used in the winter. We can ask around, but we're talking about a big area of land here.'

'Do you believe me?' asked Venus suddenly, looking at Radcliff imploringly.

Radcliff ignored the question and stood up. 'Venus, you've been through one hell of an ordeal and I'm not going to keep you up any further tonight.'

'But do you believe me?' Venus persisted.

Radcliff looked down at her. 'The facts will come out Venus – they usually do. All you need to do for now is get yourself some sleep.'

As she was saying this her mobile rang. She took the call and said 'yes' several times, before ending the call.

'Your bike's been picked up, Dennis. It's in a pretty bad way. And the poacher – Simmons – was apprehended five minutes ago, with an empty rifle and a bag full of dead chickens.'

She looked at Dennis. 'What time do you start breakfast here?'

'About eight,' Dennis replied.

'Can you keep everyone in the canteen for a bit tomorrow morning? I'll need to take a full statement from Venus.'

Dennis nodded. 'Sure.'

Radcliff raised a finger in the air. 'There is one more thing,' she said solemnly, turning back to face Venus. 'I know this will be very hard but I don't want you to mention anything about these events to the others on camp. They'll have their own ideas about the disease, and I want to keep it that way. There are connected issues that reach well beyond tonight's events. So I need this to be a complete secret.'

Venus was confused. What did Radcliff mean, *connected issues that reach well beyond tonight's events*? Why the need for secrecy?

But she said nothing.

'What if the other kids heard the explosion?' Dennis asked.

'It was a thunderstorm,' Radcliff answered quickly.

'And my disappearing act?' asked Venus. 'Jed knows about it.' She said these words with a tinge of regret.

'You had a really bad headache and went for a walk to clear your head.'

'That leaves Franco,' said Dennis.

Radcliff pondered this for a second. 'Say Franco got fed up with camp and went home.'

'But his stuff's still on his bed,' Venus pointed out.

Radcliff scribbled down something on a piece of paper. She opened the office door. 'PC Jones,' she said, poking her head outside, 'There's an outhouse beyond the site canteen. I want you to go there now. There'll probably be a laptop somewhere inside. Get it bagged. Then go to the boys' dorm and bag everything on – which bunk is it, Venus?'

'Third on the right – top bunk You'll want the green holdall with the black stripe too,' added Venus.

'Understood?' asked Radcliff.

'Ma'am,' replied Jones.

Radcliff offered her hand and Venus shook it. The DCI then squeezed Dennis on the shoulder. 'We're still on for the fifth, aren't we?'

'Wouldn't miss it,' Dennis replied.

Radcliff then strode out of the office.

'*Venus,*' said Dennis, walking over and throwing his arms around her. 'I can't believe any of this. It's so shocking.'

Venus choked back the sobs. 'I didn't mean to kill him, Granddad. I was just protecting myself.'

'I know, I know,' he said.

'What will happen to me?'

'Just do what the DCI says and it will all be OK.'

Venus looked up at him. 'Are you furious with me?'

Dennis hesitated. 'I . . . yes, I am furious with you, incredibly furious. You ignored my instructions and put your life in danger.'

Venus stared up at him, feeling guilty and devastated at the same time.

'But you've done an unbelievable thing here, Venus. You've stopped an evil attack that would have caused utter chaos. I admire you're courage and, to be honest, I'm bowled over by your persistence and commitment.'

Venus's spirits suddenly lifted a tiny bit.

'I think it will be hard for your mother to see anything positive in any of this. In fact she'd probably never let you out of the house again. And because of that we're not going to tell her about it.'

'Are you serious?' Venus was stunned. Not telling her mum about her secret stunt life was one thing, but this was totally on another planet.

'Do you honestly think we could say her one and only daughter leaped from a Cessna with a lethal canister of poison under her arm?'

Venus shook her head.

Dennis released her. 'Tonight might seem like the most shocking experience of your life, but I promise you that over time its impact will fade.'

'Really?' Venus wiped her eyes on her T-shirt.

Dennis nodded reassuringly. 'Come on.' He smiled. 'I'll walk you back to your dorm.'

When they reached the girls' dorm Dennis hugged her again and gently directed her inside. Venus crept in and made a beeline for her bunk.

The second her head touched her pillow, she fell into a deep sleep.

🏃 Chapter 41

07.45

'Has she found her mobile yet?'

'I've just got up, Gail.' Dennis rubbed his bleary eyes.

'Well, has she got it?'

'No, but don't worry. I know how expensive they are – I'll get her a new one.'

'It's not the money, Dad. It's the principle.'

'Kids lose things, love.'

'I know, but . . .'

'Go easy on her, Gail.'

'Why?'

'We – we all had a very late night. She's exhausted.'

'OK, but when she wakes up, lend her your phone and tell her to call me.'

'Will do.'

08.33

People were just finishing eating breakfast when Dennis called for quiet in the canteen. 'I've got a little stunt quiz for you. In pairs, now. The winners get a top prize.'

There were groans around the room.

'This is the prize,' Dennis explained, holding up a massive bar of chocolate.

The groans stopped immediately.

'OK. Sort yourself into pairs and we'll get cracking.'

09.30

DCI Radcliff finished writing and put her pen down. Her officers had made a start on local barns, but had so far found nothing. She was sitting opposite Venus in the site office in the same position as the night before.

'I'm going to read your statement back to you to

check it's exactly like you said,' Radcliff explained.

Venus nodded when Radcliff finished.

There was silence for a few moments.

'Before we go any further, Venus, I want you to know that Annie is going to make a full recovery. We've let Alan Docker carry on thinking it was some type of flu. He's been told that the bio-people managed to isolate the outbreak and that any risk has passed. He believes antibiotics are curing Annie and his animals. And we want to keep it that way. Like I said yesterday – I'm trusting you to keep this to yourself.'

Venus cleared her throat. 'What about Franco's death, are you . . . going to arrest me?'

Radcliff gave Venus a hard stare. 'No, Venus, I'm not going to arrest you. An investigation into the whole affair has been launched and I'm heading it. This morning, a team of officers are going to start scouring the countryside for the barn you described. I will need to talk to you again at some point.'

'So that's it?'

Radcliff nodded, stood up and walked out of the site office. Venus followed her.

'I'll be in touch,' Radcliff said, and then she hurried along the path and out of sight.

🏃 Chapter 42

09.50

Venus slipped into the canteen just as Dennis was finishing his quiz.

'Where have you been?' whispered Donna. 'I could have done with your help in the quiz.'

'Stomach-ache,' Venus replied. 'Dennis told me to go back to bed for a bit.'

'How do you feel now?'

'Yeah – loads better.'

'Excellent.' Donna grinned, and slapped Venus on the back. 'Catch you later. She joined the others, who were drifting out of the canteen.

Venus hung back with Jed. They both started speaking at the same time.

'You go first,' said Jed.

'I'm really sorry about shouting at you. I wanted to handle Franco by myself.'

'No, I'm sorry,' Jed began. 'It's just that something snapped in me.'

Venus smiled. 'Thanks. I mean, yeah, I know why you did it.'

'What happened last night?' he asked, suddenly looking very serious. 'I saw that you and Franco had both gone somewhere so I panicked. I went straight to get Dennis and he told me to wait in the site office. I was there for ages and then I heard this really loud bang, like some kind of explosion.

Venus looked surprised.

'I thought something might have happened to you,' Jed continued. 'But when Dennis finally came back he said you were OK and told me to go back to bed. It was totally weird.'

'I don't know anything about an explosion, but there was a massive storm – it must have been that,' Venus replied. 'I went for a walk. Dennis found me and gave me a lecture. That's it. And as for Franco, I haven't got a clue.'

Jed looked uncertain. 'I know it's stupid, but I'd built up this whole crazy thing that you and Franco were settling some sort of dispute. You know, with all of the tension between the two of you?'

'Don't be mad!' replied Venus, shuddering slightly. 'I've got far better things to do than settle petty disputes with Franco.'

'I haven't seen him today,' Jed added. 'Have you?'

'Nope.'

Jed still looked perplexed, but at that moment, they heard Dennis rounding the stragglers up, so they left the canteen together.

'Mum.'

'Venus, I'm so glad it's you. Dennis told me about your phone going missing.'

'I'm really sorry about it – I – I –' Venus fought back tears. Why didn't she just confess everything to her mum? How long was she going to keep these secrets and lies? They were getting bigger and more dangerous.

'What is it, honey? This hasn't got anything to do with that Franco boy has it?'

'No, Mum . . . I just got a bit upset about my mobile. And I'm really tired.'

'Dennis said you had a late night.'

'Yeah, but I feel much better now. I slept well.'

'Don't worry about the phone. We'll sort something out.'

'Thanks. Oh, and Mum …'

'Yes?'

Venus paused. 'Nothing. I'll speak to you soon.'

'OK, just take care of yourself.'

10.00

'Before we do anything today,' Dennis said to the faces in the common room, 'Lots of you have noticed that Franco's not around this morning. That's because he's left camp.'

There were a few murmurs of shock.

'Where's he gone?' asked Polly.

'He left early this morning,' Dennis continued, ignoring the question. Venus could tell he was uneasy as he spun the lie. 'He said he'd had enough. I tried to talk him round but he wasn't having it. So he took his stuff and went.'

Venus swallowed hard as she thought about the hand sticking up through the logs in the barn.

'Do you think that's true?' Donna whispered to Venus.

Venus shrugged. 'I reckon,' she replied, noticing her clammy hands and rapid heartbeat.

20.05

After supper Dennis sat everyone down on the circle of logs around the fire pit.

The last day of camp had been full-on. Dennis had suggested Venus miss the morning's quad-bike session, but she'd insisted on taking part. After lunch there had been a session on horses. As everyone had emerged from the equipment store in riding gear, Dennis had grinned at Venus.

'Fancy riding Sampson?' he asked her, leading over a gorgeous light brown horse with a white blaze on his forehead.

And Dennis managed to squeeze every last drop of energy from his charges as he'd rounded off camp with one last go on the assault course – where Venus finally managed to shave the fifteen seconds off her original time.

'Well, people, that's it,' he said, smiling. 'The stunts are over. There'll be a party tonight and in the morning you'll all be gone. You've been an excellent group, really excellent, and I promise you I can't say that to every group I've had here. I can see that quite a few of you are very serious about becoming stunt artists.'

Jed winked at Venus.

'To those people, I say this: the stunt world is as hard as any other part of the film industry to break into, possibly harder because there aren't that many of us qualified to do it. If you do want to make the grade, you need to be totally single-minded and completely determined. Despite all of the pressures and difficulties, if you do succeed, it's a pretty good means of earning a living. So if you see yourself heading that way, then I wish you immense luck and you never know – our paths might cross again, professionally. Now, go back to your dorms, clean the mud of your faces and get ready to party.'

There was a spontaneous round of clapping and several cheers for Dennis. He waved this away and went off to get bin bags. As everyone trailed off, Venus spotted Alan Docker walking towards the site office hand-in-hand with a young girl. Her hair was in blond ringlets and a cheeky smile was on her lips.

Venus stared. It must be Annie. She realised, *If I hadn't acted, she probably wouldn't be here.*

 Chapter 43

21.15

For the party Venus wore a black mini-skirt, a red halterneck top and matching strappy heels. Jed and the others couldn't disguise their surprise when she walked into the common room.

'Wow, Venus,' Jed whispered. 'You look amazing!'

The party kicked off with a show compèred by Donna. Venus was one of the star turns, with her impression of Dennis. Most people completely cracked up and even Dennis managed a giggle or two. The show was followed by food and dancing. After a couple of hours, Venus found herself sitting with Jed on the steps outside the back of the canteen.

'I can't believe it's over,' Venus said.

'Me too,' Jed replied, 'it's been so good – the stunts, the laughs – the getting to know you.'

Venus felt her cheeks redden a fraction.

Jed slipped his arm around Venus's shoulder but at that second, Polly and Cleo burst round the corner, shrieking with laughter. They stopped when they saw the scene in front of them. Jed immediately took his arm away from Venus's shoulder and Venus stood up.

'Oh,' said Cleo, with raised eyebrows, 'we didn't realise –'

'It's cool,' said Venus. 'I need a drink anyway.'

Polly and Cleo ran off. Venus and Jed walked back to the common room.

Most people were in there, lying on the sofas, crying with laughter about the funniest moments from the last ten days. Venus and Jed joined them for a bit. When Venus said she was tired, Jed offered to walk her back to the girls' dorm.

As they stood outside, their shadows stretched across the side of the building.

'All right?' Jed asked.

'Totally.' Venus smiled. She kissed him on the cheek and went inside.

23.06

Long after the party was finished, Dennis stood in the heart of the wood.

He enjoyed the still silence for a few seconds and

then pulled the light blue envelope out of his jacket. He must have read it over a hundred times by now, but however much he hoped for a new meaning, it always conveyed the same message. He couldn't put things off for ever. He pulled a box from his trousers and lit a match – watching the flames curl up and over the letter, hungrily swallowing the paper and ink.

Dennis punctured the centre of the letter with a thin twig and he waited until every last scrap had been completely transformed to ash. When there was no trace whatsoever remaining, he dropped the twig on the floor and stamped out the already fading amber glow.

He gave it one last look and headed back to his cabin.

DAY ELEVEN

🏃 Chapter 44

10.16

The final few hours were pretty rushed. Dennis organised a massive clear-up of the site and then spent a few hours ferrying people between departure points.

Half the group was taken to the bus depot. Jed, Donna, Tariq and Steve were catching a train up north; Venus, Polly and Spike were heading back to London. At the station Donna gave Venus a huge bear hug. 'Phone me when you get back from France,' she insisted. 'I want all of the gossip.' Venus had exchanged phone numbers with most people by the second night of camp.

Venus laughed. 'You'll get it all,' she said, beaming, and she punched Donna affectionately on the arm of her leather jacket.

Then Jed walked over. 'It . . . it's been amazing!' He laughed.

'The most unbelievable ten days of my life!' Venus grinned. 'Call me,' she added.

Jed pretended to think about this for a moment. 'You know, I think I might.' He laughed. 'Maybe you can come up and visit sometime – half-term, Christmas, something like that?'

'Definitely!' Venus nodded.

He hugged her tightly. 'I'm going to really miss you,' he whispered into her ear.

'Farewells over,' called Dennis.

Venus and Jed parted and looked at each other. Dennis hurried over, quickly shook hands with Jed, Donna and the other northerners and told them to head for their platform.

Venus watched them as they walked off. Just before they turned the corner, Jed turned back and waved at Venus.

Dennis then slapped Spike on the back and shook hands with Polly and Venus. 'Now it's your turn,' he said.

He walked the three of them over to their platform. The train was just pulling in. Spike and Polly got on.

'What can I say, Venus?' Dennis said, smiling, as he pulled her towards him for a hug.

'Thanks for everything, Granddad,' Venus said, as tears rolled down her face.

'Hey, kid.' He pulled back and looked at his granddaughter.

'See you back home,' he whispered, 'and don't worry about anything. It's all going to be fine.'

Venus dried the tears with her hands. 'You're amazing, Granddad.' She smiled.

A whistle sounded further up the platform.

'Get on that train now!' Dennis commanded. 'Or you'll have to come back to the site with me and do the assault course again.'

Venus laughed and climbed on.

15.06

After Venus's train pulled into Euston, she said goodbye to Polly and Spike.

When she looked up, she saw her mum walking briskly along the platform. Part of her wanted to run into her mum's arms like a tiny kid and tell her everything she'd been through. But she made herself put on a calm exterior as Gail approached, hugged her tightly and picked up her bag.

'Welcome home, honey. What happened to your cheek?'

'Just an accident.' Venus smiled.

'So?' asked Gail. 'How was it?'

Venus thought about this for a few seconds. 'It was

pretty eventful, Mum, but I lied about something.'

Gail pulled a face.

'The food,' said Venus.

'Oh yes?'

'It was rubbish.'

16.00

As Gail opened the front door, Venus smelled the homely aroma of food wafting through the house. But her eyes were closing heavily as she dropped her bag in the hallway.

'I think I'll crash now for a couple of hours and then eat, if that's OK?'

'Of course it is,' replied Gail. 'You need it.'

Venus shut her bedroom door and got out the grainy black and white photo from her cupboard. She lay on her bed twisting it in her hands. All of the usual questions swirled around her head as she stared into her father's eyes.

When I get back from France I'm going to start looking for some serious answers, she promised herself.

She fell asleep with the photo tucked under her pillow.

DAY TWELVE

🏃 Chapter 45

09.00

Venus slept for fifteen hours.

When she finally woke up she was seriously hungry. She ate a massive breakfast that was punctuated by a call from Dennis. Gail spoke to him first and then passed him over. Venus took the phone into the living room.

'Everything OK?' he asked.

'Yeah,' Venus replied. 'Any news from Radcliff?'

'No,' answered Dennis, 'but I told you it will be fine.'

Venus was tempted to ask Dennis about how he knew Radcliff, but she reckoned she wouldn't get any more information out of him, so she left it – for the moment.

'Anyway,' said Dennis, 'have a brilliant time in France. And don't go attempting any more heroics.'

'Don't worry,' Venus reassured him.

As she put the phone down and turned around Venus saw her mum standing in the doorway.

'Who's Radcliff?' asked Gail.

Venus felt a twitch in her chest. 'Just a friend at stunt camp' she replied.

'Girl or boy?'

'Er . . . girl.'

'What news are you expecting from her?'

'It's just a kick-boxing thing mum, nothing important.'

Gail shrugged, but didn't move for a second – she knew when her daughter was holding something back from her, but she let it go.

10.24

The Springs' hallway was cluttered with bags.

Gail and Kate's mum Sonya had started packing their stuff into the car. Kate was looking for her iPod.

Venus went to the kitchen to grab an apple and as she came back, her mum was flicking through a small bundle of letters the postman had just handed her.

'This one's for you,' she said, handing over a postcard.

Venus bit into the apple and studied the front of the card. It was one of those cheesy London sight-seeing highlights postcards, split into quarters: Big Ben; the Tower of London; Nelson's Column and the Houses of Parliament. She shrugged and turned it over.

Instantly every ounce of life drained from her cheeks.

Gail and Sonya were out front, shuffling cases around in the boot of the car.

'Are you OK?' asked Kate, wandering in and noticing the horrified expression on Venus's face.

Venus held the postcard in her hand as if it was a bomb about to detonate. It contained three words.

See you soon.

It was dated yesterday morning and had been sent from a central London postcode. She immediately recognised the long spindly writing.

It was from Franco.

Acknowledgements

I owe a huge debt of thanks to top British stuntwoman Sarah Franzl, who acted as my consultant for this book. Sarah's information, insights and advice were totally invaluable when it came to researching the stunt world, and she was very generous with her time. Whenever I see a film containing one of the stunts she's performed, I'm bowled over by her bravery and determination. She's an amazing woman.

Sarah has worked on an huge variety of films and TV shows, from *Harry Potter* movies to *EastEnders*. She has doubled (done the stunt scenes for) many of the film world's biggest stars, including Kate Winslet in *Titanic*. Sarah performed the dangerous scenes in *Titanic* – like rushing along a deck with thousands of gallons of water cascading down on her. When Sarah's scenes had been filmed, her head was edited out and replaced by Kate Winslet's head. So, when you see the film, it looks like Kate Winslet is running along the deck nearly drowning, whereas it's actually Sarah.

Next time you see a film, check out the stunt artists who are credited at the end. These people don't share any of the limelight with the stars they double for. Yet, day in day out, they risk serious injury and often their lives, to deliver jaw-dropping scenes for us, the viewing public. They're an incredible group of people.

I also want to thank Brenda Gardner at Piccadilly for seeing the potential in Venus and agreeing to publish this book; my brilliant editor, Jon Appleton, who enormously helped me in shaping this project; Melissa Patey, for always being totally helpful and making things happen, and the rest of the Piccadilly team; Janice Swanson at Curtis Brown for making me focus; Dawn Gobourne for her great support and kindness and all of the crew at AP library; Alison Goodman and Anne Joseph for their proofing and very wise comments; Sophie Lansman and Jason Kelvin – the visual wizards; William and Rachel Bowley for reading and commenting on the early drafts; Big Dave C for his intelligent and insightful comments; And above all, Fi, for her enduring encouragement and sense of humour when I was talking about, planning and writing this book.

www.piccadillypress.co.uk

☆ The latest news on forthcoming books

☆ Chapter previews

☆ Author biographies

☆ Fun quizzes

☆ Reader reviews

☆ Competitions and fab prizes

☆ Book features and cool downloads

☆ And much, much more . . .

Log on and check it out!

Piccadilly Press